Lights,
Music,
Code!

by Jo Whittemore

Penguin Workshop
An Imprint of Penguin Random House

PENGUIN WORKSHOP
Penguin Young Readers Group
An Imprint of Penguin Random House LLC

Text and cover illustration copyright © 2018 by Penguin Random House LLC and Girls Who Code Inc. All rights reserved. Published by Penguin Workshop, an imprint of Penguin Random House LLC, 345 Hudson Street, New York, New York 10014. PENGUIN and PENGUIN WORKSHOP are trademarks of Penguin Books Ltd, and the W colophon is a trademark of Penguin Random House LLC. Printed in the USA.

Emoji © denisgorelkin/Thinkstock.

Library of Congress Cataloging-in-Publication Data is available.

ISBN 9780399542534   10 9 8 7 6 5 4 3 2 1

Hi, I'm Reshma. I'm the founder of Girls Who Code, where we teach middle- and high-school girls how to change the world by writing code and creating digital games, apps, websites, and more.

Have you been to a school dance yet? What was it like, or what do you think it'll be like? I remember my first one like it was yesterday. It was in the middle-school gym in my hometown in Illinois. I wore a flower-print dress and jelly bracelets on my wrists, and I crimped my hair (believe it or not, that was a cool style back then). I went with a group of my girlfriends, and we danced to our favorite songs. It was a blast—and the best part was being there with my closest friends.

Reading this book took me right back to that night. In these pages, you'll learn about Maya and her friends in coding club, and a big project they're working on—coding the lights and music for their school dance! But then an old friend of Maya's comes to town and causes trouble. I was on the edge of my seat wondering whether Maya and her friends would rally together for the big night—and you will be, too.

We used one of my favorite examples of coding in this book: wearables! Wearables are electronic devices—like fitness trackers or hearing aids—that you wear on your body. You can do amazing things with wearable technology, like sew light sensors into a dress and program them to light up to the beat of music. Fashion models have worn some of these "smart" dresses on runways all around the world. In fact, one of our alumni helped create the technology that powered the first-ever LED dress at New York Fashion Week. Pretty cool!

If you like reading this book, I hope you'll join one of our free coding clubs across the country. In our clubs, you can explore coding your own wearables and hang out with girls who will become some of your best friends.

Happy reading—and coding!

Reshma Saujani

Chapter One

"Maya, you are seriously looking fierce," I said, pointing at my reflection.

She smiled at the compliment.

Either that or she was hoping I'd finally pick an outfit after ten costume changes. I'd bought a killer top over the weekend, and it *begged* for the perfect shoes and skirt. They were just taking forever to find.

I wasn't being picky out of shallowness. I actually had good reasons to worry about my appearance:

1. I was the fashion columnist for my school paper and needed to look the part.
2. It was Monday, and Mondays were bad enough without adding sweatpants.
3. My friends and I had just made it onto the

local news, which meant all eyes would be on us for the next few days. Loop to reason one.

I decided to stick with my last combo: gray leggings and a plum-colored skirt paired with my lemon-yellow top. I added rain boots in the same yellow to pull it all together. The bright colors were a little daring, and my nails would've looked better with purple polish than with pink, but fashion is all about risk. Plus, I'd just spent ten minutes in front of my bedroom mirror and was about to miss the school bus.

I tossed my less-than-perfect clothing options in the closet and caught my reflection in several more mirrors... tiny ones I'd sewn into a dress. My school was having a dance on Saturday, and the theme (thought up by yours truly) was "The Future Is ..." So I'd bought a bag of craft mirrors and painstakingly stitched them onto an old white sundress I had. I got the idea from a mirror-covered dress I'd seen at the mall.

It would've been easier to buy the store version, but there was no way my parents would give me the money. Why? Because they still liked to remind me of the last time they paid for something of mine. It had caused a sticky situation, literally and figuratively. And it was also the reason I didn't wear purple nail polish anymore.

See, I have a big secret I haven't told even my closest friends. Because if they—or anyone else—knew, they'd never look at me the same.

The fact is that I, Maya Chung, am a former shoplifter.

Well, a one-time, *unsuccessful* former shoplifter.

Crazy, right? You wouldn't think it to look at me, but it's true.

And it's all because of Nicole Davis, a girl I became friends with over the summer. She was visiting her aunts who live down the street from my family, and since we were so close in age, one of Nicole's aunts suggested we hang out together.

Things started out great. Every time I saw Nicole, she had a new pair of earrings or a cool top to show off. She'd even let me borrow her stuff for days at a time. But then I found out how she'd gotten these newfound treasures: She'd stolen them.

And the "borrowing" she'd let me do? It was to keep the items out of her house so her aunts wouldn't notice them. Pretty tricky, right? Even worse, she got me to try shoplifting!

Emphasis on the word *try.*

I may have toppled a nail polish display while sneaking a bottle of Purple Rain into my purse.

My mom and stepdad, Oliver, were furious, and they had to pay for all the nail polishes I'd broken. Needless to say, asking them for money before I turned eighty was out of the question.

"Maya, I hear the bus coming!" Oliver shouted upstairs.

Giving my reflection one last glance, I slung my backpack over one shoulder and hurried down.

"Goodbye, parental units. I love you and beg you not to wave from the porch." I paused to kiss Mom on the cheek, and she looked me over with a frown.

"Turn around, honey."

"What?" I spun in a circle. "What's wrong?"

Mom reached behind me and tugged at the back of my blouse. She held out her hand, showing me the price tag she'd removed. "Is this new?"

I recognized that tone. What she really meant was, "Did you pay for this?"

You try to steal one measly polish, and they never let you hear the end of it.

"I bought it with my birthday money," I replied in a tone that really said, "Yes, *Mother*."

She smiled and patted my back. "It's very pretty."

4

"I thought so, too," I said. "When I *paid for it.*" I emphasized the last words so she'd get the point.

Mom chuckled and raised her hands in surrender. "Okay, okay." She glanced at Oliver, who was watching us with a blank expression.

Oliver and my mom have been together for as long as I can remember (my biological dad passed away when I was four), but he still tries to stay out of mother-daughter arguments. A smart choice, in my opinion.

"You know what's not okay?" He pointed toward the front door and, on cue, an engine rumbled outside, followed by a long, loud honk.

The bus. Never had I been so happy to leave for school.

I ran to the door, but once I opened it, I slowed my pace and strode confidently down the driveway. Nobody respected the word of a frantic fashion columnist.

The bus driver gestured for me to hurry, but I flicked the ends of my hair and didn't break my stride. Oliver's the head chef of a fancy restaurant, and he says if you act confident, you'll feel confident. It's pretty good advice, coming from a man who wears white sneakers with black socks.

"Glad you could grace us with your presence, Miss Chung," the bus driver said as I stepped on board.

I smiled at him and took my seat next to Erin, who grinned when she saw me.

"Good. Morning. Maya," she said in a robotic voice, moving her arms and head in mechanical jerks.

My smile deepened. "Hello. Erin!" I said in my own robot voice. "Do. You. Have. Any. Oil?"

We both giggled. Everyone in earshot gave us strange looks. But then, they hadn't been talking like robots like we had when preparing for the hackathon for coding club.

Erin and I were both members of coding club, along with our friends Lucy, Sophia, and Leila. They're the close friends I mentioned to whom I can't tell my secret. They were also the ones I'd recently been on the news with because of the hackathon we competed in. It's like a marathon but for computer programming, where everyone uses their coding skills. This one involved robots, and we programmed ours to dance—kind of by mistake, though.

Mrs. Clark, our advisor, was there, too, and even though we didn't win first place, she couldn't stop gushing about how proud of us she was. When my team was awarded a tour of a local programming company, she actually jumped up and down. I've never seen a teacher do that, except Mr. Robard, my newspaper advisor, when he saw a rat. He jumped up on his desk pretty fast, but the coming-down part took a while.

Erin shifted her bag. "Cute top! Is it new?"

I reminded myself not to use the same annoyed tone I did with my mother. Erin didn't know about my fifteen-second life of crime.

"It is! I bought it with my birthday money," I said.

"I wish I could spend the money my dad sends on whatever *I* want." Erin made a face. Her parents got divorced not long ago, so she lives with her mom now.

"Your mom doesn't let you spend your own money?" I asked.

"No, she chooses something cheap and then puts the rest in savings." Erin rolled her eyes to the top of her blue-framed glasses. "Clearly my mom's forgotten how rich I'll be when Hollywood calls." She made a ringing sound and held her phone to her ear. "Hello? You guys need me for *another* billion-dollar film?" Erin held her hand over the phone and whispered, "Sorry, I have to take this."

I laughed and shook my head. She jokes about it, but Erin is definitely Hollywood material. She can sing, she's an awesome actress, and she can do so many impersonations, it's like talking to twenty people instead of one.

"Sorry your mom isn't cool about money," I said.

"Oh, not just money. My life!" Erin rolled her eyes. "She wants to chaperone at the dance."

"Seriously?" I was in charge of the dance, and so far none of my friends' parents had signed up to chaperone. My mom couldn't because she had a work event (she was in charge of marketing for a local advertising company), and I'd convinced Oliver not to by promising to wash his car every week for a month. "Does your mom want to check up on you?" I gasped and grabbed Erin's arm. "Did someone ask you to the dance?"

Erin shook her head. "Not yet, but who knows? Maybe I'll ask someone myself. The idea has been *dancing* through my head since Sophia asked Sammy." She elbowed me and grinned.

"Ugh. You're so cheesy, it's making me lactose intolerant," I said, wrinkling my nose.

Erin laughed. "That was a gouda one. Get it? Good-a? Gouda?"

I clapped my hand to my forehead. "I've created a muenster!"

We traded cheese-related puns and then cracker-related puns until the bus pulled up to the school.

"Wait, I've got one more," said Erin, giggling as she stepped off the bus. "How—"

"Finally!" Lucy ran toward us as soon as our feet touched the pavement. Her braids bounced with each step. "Where have you guys *been*?"

"Um . . ." I turned and pointed to the bus behind us.

While I have trouble keeping track of time, Lucy's the opposite. She's always ready to go and always wants results *now*. She expected to design an app on the first day of coding club, even though apps can take years to perfect. Sometimes her impatience can be a little frustrating, but she does keep our group on track, so I can't stay mad.

"What's the big rush?" I asked.

"Yeah, it's Monday morning," said Erin. "Nothing school-related could've happened in the past two days."

"Mrs. Clark wanted to see us before homeroom, remember?" Lucy prompted. "To take a photo for the paper?"

Erin and I exchanged panicked glances.

"I completely forgot!"

"Me too!"

"Well, come on!" Lucy tugged at our hands. "Sophia and Leila are already waiting."

The three of us hurried into the building (FYI, it is *not* easy to run in rain boots) and down the hall to the computer lab.

"We're here!" Erin gasped, doubling over. "We made it."
She dropped to the carpet and sprawled out. "Feel free to
pose around me."

"Oh my," said Mrs. Clark.

The newspaper photographer snapped a picture of Erin.

Sophia raised an eyebrow. "Where did you guys run
from—Alaska?"

"The . . . school . . . bus," I said, taking a deep breath.

Sophia whistled. "We have *got* to work on your cardio."

Of all my friends, Sophia is the most athletic. She plays
softball and even manages the boys' football team.

"Thank you, girls, for getting here so quickly," said Mrs.
Clark. "Along with the photos, the newspaper would like
to run a small article on you. I hope that's okay."

For me, it wasn't a big deal since I work at the school
paper, but my friends were gasping and squealing with
delight.

"That's totally okay!" said Lucy.

Melanie Eastwick, a reporter for our hometown
newspaper, leaped up from where she'd been sitting. She
wore a fedora with a card that said PRESS sticking out of
the brim. The woman clearly took her job very seriously.

She approached Leila first, pen poised over her notepad,
while the photographer hovered between them. Leila

adjusted her head scarf and tried to act casual.

"First of all," said Melanie, "I think it's awesome what the five of you are doing for girlkind everywhere."

Leila frowned. "Girlkind? Is that even a word?"

"It will be once the Oxford English Dictionary gets my petition," Melanie said with a wink. "Now, are you in this to prove that girls do, in fact, rule while boys drool?"

Mrs. Clark cleared her throat. "Melanie, we don't compete to prove girls are better than boys or vice versa. We do it to show that *anyone* can excel in STEAM, regardless of gender, education, or race."

It was true. Sophia, Lucy, and I hadn't known any coding before this year, while Erin and Leila had at least a little background. And when it came to embracing races, Sophia was Latina, Lucy was African American, I was Chinese, Leila was Pakistani, and Erin was white.

"STEAM's definitely for everyone," I agreed.

Melanie scribbled on her notepad. "And STEAM is...?"

"It stands for science, technology, engineering, arts, and mathematics," Erin supplied. "It's an acronym."

"Got it," said Melanie. "Now, which of you made the robot dance? That was brilliant!" She waved her pen for emphasis.

My friends and I looked at one another.

"We all kind of did," said Lucy.

"Yeah," said Sophia. "I mean, we each came up with a different part of it, but it took us all to make it work."

"Gotcha," said Melanie. "There's no *me* in team, right?"

Leila wrinkled her forehead. "Well . . . the *letters* for *me* are in team. I think you mean *I*."

Melanie frowned. "No. There's no *i* in team."

"That's what . . ." Leila's forehead wrinkled even further, and I squeezed her shoulder.

"Just let it go," I whispered.

On the floor beside me, Erin giggled.

Erin, Lucy, Sophia, and I actually met Leila after her hackathon teammates dropped out, leaving her to compete alone. We invited her to join us—we knew she was really good at robotics—and she turned out to be a really great friend, too.

Melanie asked a few more questions and then nodded to the photographer. "Time for pictures!"

My friends and I posed on either side of Mrs. Clark. After the photographer had sufficiently blinded us with the camera flash, he and Melanie left the computer lab.

"I just want to say again how proud I am of you girls," said Mrs. Clark, while the rest of us gathered our things. "That was a tough competition, and earning a tour of

TechTown was a huge accomplishment."

My friends and I grinned at one another.

"Maybe we can improve our robot design in coding club today," Leila said hopefully.

Mrs. Clark put a hand on her shoulder. "I'm always for improvement, but I've already got something in mind for this afternoon. And it includes"—she lowered her voice and looked around conspiratorially—"a surprise."

Sophia and I *ooh*ed. Lucy gasped and clasped her hands together, and Leila and Erin ventured guesses.

"Can we eat the surprise?"

"Do we get to make a video game?"

Mrs. Clark laughed. "No to both. You'll have to wait and find out!"

The first bell rang, and Mrs. Clark ushered us into the hall. "See you this afternoon!" she called.

"What do you think the surprise is?" Lucy asked the rest of us as we gathered outside the computer lab.

"Whatever it is, it's big enough for everyone in the club. Otherwise, she would've said 'a surprise for one of you,'" Leila pointed out.

"That's true. But what would we find surprising?" asked Erin.

"If the cafeteria used real beef," said Sophia.

The rest of us giggled.

"Well, Mrs. Clark's a fun teacher, so whatever it is will be fun, too," I said.

Since we didn't have long before the warning bell, Lucy, Sophia, and Leila hurried off to their homerooms. Mine was just across the hall, so I hung back with Erin, who was getting a drink of water.

"I hope the surprise is money," I said, leaning against the wall.

"That'd be nice," she said. "Then I could buy some clothes *I* chose, instead of wearing what my mom picks." She gestured to my outfit. "You're lucky your mom has good taste."

I laughed. "She didn't pick these pieces. I did."

Erin's jaw dropped. "Your mom buys whatever you want?"

"No!" I laughed harder. "I got most of these myself."

"How can you afford them?" She narrowed her eyes. "Do you steal them? Maya Chung, are you a fashion thief?"

I knew she was kidding, but I couldn't help stiffening and scowling. "No. I'm not."

Erin's eyes widened, and she reached for my shoulder. "That was totally a joke. I didn't mean it."

I relaxed. "Good. Because everything I own is bought and paid for."

Erin nodded so hard her glasses slid down her nose. "Absolutely."

"Hey, Maya?" A student office aide approached us. "The principal wants to see you."

I stiffened again, this time in fear. "The principal? Are you sure she meant me?"

He snorted. "Is there another Maya Chung?"

I looked at Erin, who shrugged. "Maybe you're getting some sort of Best Dressed award."

"Yeah, maybe," I said doubtfully. "I'll see you later," I told her and followed the office aide, my heartbeat almost as fast and loud as the thrum of the tardy bell.

Principal Stephens's voice was light when I knocked on her door, which I took as a good sign.

"Come in," she said.

I pushed it open just enough to poke my head through. "You wanted to see me?"

"Yes!" Principal Stephens gestured for me to step forward. "We have a new student starting today, and I was hoping you could show her around campus. I hear you're old friends."

I opened the door wider and saw who was sitting across from Principal Stephens.

It was Nicole Davis—the shoplifter.

$\mathcal{I}$ stared at Nicole, openmouthed and aware that so far my only greeting had been, "Uhhh."

"Maya, hi! It's so great to see you!" Nicole stepped forward and flung her arms around me. She must have forgotten how she ran when I got caught in the Great Nail Polish Heist.

"Uhhh," I began again, but this time I followed it with a friendly greeting. "Why are you here?"

(Hey, I didn't say, "Why are you here, *jerk*?" See? Friendly.)

Nicole pulled away, still smiling. "To go to school, silly! My parents just bought a house near my aunts."

"Oh." I nodded. "Cool."

Nicole finally picked up on my lack of enthusiasm and furrowed her eyebrows. "*I* thought it was."

Principal Stephens handed Nicole's schedule to me.

"Could you walk Miss Davis to her locker and show her where her classes are?"

"Of course," I told Principal Stephens. Then I looked at Nicole. "Are you ready?"

"Almost." She picked up her bag and extended a hand to Principal Stephens. "Thank you for welcoming me to your school."

I raised an eyebrow. Who was this girl? The Nicole I knew had stuck her tongue out at a lifeguard who told her to stop running at the pool.

The principal chuckled and shook Nicole's hand. "My door is always open to you."

My former partner-in-crime turned to me, grinning once more. "Let's do this!"

Principal Stephens thanked me, and I held the door open for Nicole.

"The seventh-grade lockers are near the cafeteria," I said. "Let's check them out first."

The door closed behind us, and Nicole grabbed my arm. "Maya, please don't be mad. I'm sorry for getting you in trouble this summer. I shouldn't have run away and left you alone."

I faced her. "No, you shouldn't have talked me into it to begin with! Now, because of you, my mom barely trusts me."

"I'm sorry!" She held up her hands. "Look, I screwed up, but I've learned my lesson. I told my parents everything and even made them ground me and take my phone for the rest of the summer."

My eyebrows lifted. "Really?"

"Yes! That's why I never called to apologize."

"Huh." That made me feel a little better.

"And I can prove I've changed." Nicole fumbled through her purse and pulled out a tiny slip of paper. "Here."

I smoothed it out. "A receipt for gum. Wow, it's almost like having the real thing."

"No, the point is that I *paid* for the gum," she said. "The old me would've just taken it!"

That was true.

"But I do have gum if you want." She pawed through her purse again and took out a stick. When I reached for it, she held on, her eyes meeting mine. "This is a peace offering, Maya. I will be a better friend this time. I promise."

She looked sincere and really seemed like she'd changed. Plus the gum was my favorite flavor: strawberry. I couldn't say no.

"Okay," I said, taking it. "But you do know the typical peace offering is an olive branch, right?"

"I'm sorry," she said with a solemn nod. "I couldn't fit one in my purse."

I stared at her for a moment, and then we both burst out laughing.

"I'm so glad we're friends again!" Nicole linked her arm through mine.

"I know, but we'd better find your classes and your locker," I said, checking her schedule. "It looks like you'll be by my friend Erin."

"Fun! I can't wait to meet all your friends," Nicole gushed. "Can I eat lunch with you guys?"

"Sure, they don't really . . ." I trailed off.

I'd been about to say, "They don't really know what I did over the summer," but then I realized: What if Nicole blurted it before I had a chance to explain myself?

"You know, I just remembered I have to meet with them about coding club at lunch today. But how about tomorrow?" I asked.

"Great!" said Nicole. "And maybe you and I can catch up after school?"

"Oh! Actually, I have a coding club . . . uh . . . meeting then," I said, realizing how dumb it sounded.

Nicole noticed, too. "So you have to meet your coding-club friends at lunch before you meet them later in coding club?"

"Yeah," I said. "Because we're . . . we're going to talk about what we're doing in coding club."

"Or you're going to tell them about me before you introduce me," she said with a smirk.

Busted.

I put my hands to my quickly reddening cheeks. "Is it possible for someone's face to catch *fire*?"

Nicole laughed. "Maya, it's fine. I get it. Just promise you'll tell them as much good stuff about me as bad."

"I promise," I said.

But later, when I met my friends for lunch, I didn't find myself talking about Nicole at all. Mainly because Erin had splayed her upper body across the table and was lamenting about the dance.

"I was going to wear my hula skirt, but now that he's asked, what am I supposed to wear?" she groaned.

"Why a hula skirt?" I asked. "And why can't you still wear it?"

"Who are you going with?" Leila asked.

Erin looked from one of us to the other. I pointed to Leila.

"Her question is better. Answer hers first."

"Jeremiah Whitley asked me," Erin said, sitting up straight.

"The cute guy with the mohawk?" asked Sophia.

Erin nodded. "And after I said yes, he told me his costume. It clearly doesn't go with my hula skirt."

"But why a hula skirt?" I asked again. "The theme is the future."

"That's what I see myself wearing in the future," said Erin. "When I'm a professional hula dancer."

"I thought you wanted to be an actress," said Leila.

"I can do both," she said, nodding to me. "Maya gives fashion advice and writes code. Two completely different things."

"You can't argue with logic like that," I said.

"Right! So what am I supposed to do?" asked Erin.

"Be happy you're going with someone." Lucy stabbed her juice box with a straw.

"But what am I supposed to wear?" She turned to Sophia. "You're going with Sammy, right? What are you wearing?"

"Does it really matter? It's just a stupid dance," she grumbled.

The rest of us stared at her.

Lucy cleared her throat. "So enough of *that* subject. Maya, who was that girl you were walking with between classes? I've never seen her before."

Erin shook herself out of her funk. "Yeah, is she why the principal wanted to see you?"

They were, of course, talking about Nicole. It was time to come clean.

"Nicole's someone from my past," I said.

As soon as the words came out, I realized how ridiculous I sounded.

"Ohh, your past. That clears it right up," said Sophia. "You know, since we just met this year."

Leila elbowed her. "I like how Maya says so mysteriously: 'Someone from my past.' You know this is gonna be juicy."

All my friends leaned closer to me.

I took a deep breath. "There was a time when I had a bit of a wild side."

Erin gasped. "Did you wear stripes with plaids?"

The rest of us giggled.

"No! I met Nicole this past summer, and, well, she was a bit of a troublemaker," I told them. "She's a better person now, but at the time she convinced me to do something I'm not very proud of."

My friends were hanging on my every word.

"I ..." Suddenly I couldn't look any of them in the eye. So I stared at the napkin I was shredding. "I shoplifted."

Nobody spoke for a moment, and when I glanced up, they were all staring openmouthed.

"You stole something?" asked Lucy.

I cringed. Lucy once told me she admired me, and here I was, setting the worst example.

"I *tried* to steal something—a stupid bottle of nail polish," I said, "but the security guard caught me, and my parents know, and I totally learned my lesson." I realized I was talking fast, but I couldn't stop. "Trust me; I'm more ashamed of myself than you guys are of me."

Erin put a hand on top of mine. "Everybody makes mistakes."

I shook my head. "I'm not talking about something small, like forgetting your homework."

"Neither am I," she said. "My mom absolutely forbids me from buying self-tanner, but one time I did it anyway."

Sophia snorted. "And you thought she wouldn't notice once you showed up with an insta-tan?"

"Oh, I didn't get a tan," Erin said with a smile. "I spilled half the bottle on the carpet, and my mom caught me trying to clean it up."

The rest of us made sounds of despair.

"The worst part was that I'd already put some of it on my palms before I spilled, and I didn't wash up in time."

I clapped a hand over my mouth.

"Nooo!" said Leila.

Erin held up her hands. "My palms were neon orange for

two weeks, and my mom made me wear gloves around the house."

Everyone at the table cracked up.

Erin bumped me. "So yeah, you're not the only one who makes big mistakes. And we don't think any less of you when you *do*."

Leila signaled us all to stop laughing and said, "My parents had this really expensive vase on a pedestal at our house. Nobody was allowed to touch it, so I thought it would be the perfect place to hide my Halloween candy from my sister and brother."

"Oh no!" squealed Lucy, covering her face.

Leila grinned. "You can already guess that I broke the vase." She held up a finger. "But then I put my sister's goldfish bowl on the pedestal and blamed the fish!"

We all started laughing again, and Erin had to take a drink when she started to cough.

Lucy waved her hand. "I've got one! I've got one!"

"Not sweet, innocent Lucy!" I exclaimed in mock surprise.

She blushed but told her story. "You know how the tooth fairy leaves money when your teeth fall out?"

"You're still losing teeth?" Erin asked with a deadpan expression.

Lucy pinched her. "You know what I mean! Anyway, I

thought *Forget waiting for all my teeth to fall out...*"

"Oh God, you pulled them out yourself," said Sophia with a horrified gasp.

The rest of us squealed and hid our faces.

"No!" Lucy said with a laugh. "I took modeling clay and made a bunch of fake teeth and put one under my pillow each night."

"Oh, that's clever!" said Leila.

"Did your parents fall for it?" I asked.

"At first," said Lucy with a sheepish grin. "But then I got greedy and put five teeth under my pillow at once."

"Awww," said Sophia, shaking her head.

"Greed'll get you every time," said Erin.

"What happened?" asked Leila.

"When I woke up, the teeth were still there, along with a note that said, 'You're going to the dentist tomorrow.'"

We all booed. Then Sophia started to share her story. Before she could get to the worst part, she stopped and smiled at someone behind me.

"Hi! You must be Nicole."

I turned, and sure enough, Nicole was beaming at us all and carrying a lunch tray.

"I know you guys are in the middle of coding stuff, but I just wanted to say hi. Hi!"

My friends chorused their hellos, and Nicole looked at me.

"Do you think you might be free tonight after coding club? I'd love to catch up."

Had she asked that morning, I would've said no, but after sharing my past with friends who made me feel better with their own stories, I realized Erin had been right. Everybody makes mistakes, and I shouldn't think less of Nicole for it, especially since she'd admitted she was wrong.

"Sure," I said. "I'll text you after school."

"Great—talk to you later! It was nice meeting all of you!" She waved, and my friends waved back.

"She seems nice," said Lucy.

"Yeah," said Leila, watching Nicole walk away. "Doesn't really seem like a troublemaker."

"People can surprise you," I said. Then I grinned at Sophia. "Speaking of which, what exactly did you do to that Christmas display you were telling us about?"

And soon she had the rest of us roaring with laughter.

Chapter Three

*T*here's nothing quite as disappointing as being promised a surprise only to walk in and find a perfectly normal classroom waiting for you. After sharing our stories, my friends and I had spent the rest of lunch guessing what Mrs. Clark had planned. Finally the big moment arrived, and it was . . . desks arranged in groups, as usual.

"Well, this is underwhelming," said Sophia, looking around. "Where's the confetti cannon?"

"And the balloon drop?" added Erin.

We all looked up at the ceiling.

"Oh, *there's* my pencil." Sophia pointed to half a No. 2 lodged in a ceiling tile.

"Confetti and a balloon drop are messy. The mayor's obviously bringing the keys to the city," said Lucy.

"Guys, I think this is it," said Leila, gesturing around us with a frown. "So much for my chocolate fountain."

I didn't respond. All their ideas were a little far-fetched. Clearly, Mrs. Clark was taking us on a shopping spree.

My friends and I sat and watched other students file in. Each one glanced around, too, with disappointed expressions. When Mrs. Clark finally appeared, she turned off the lights and pressed a button to lower the projector screen at the front of the room.

"Sweet! Movie time in coding club," Bradley said.

"Good afternoon, everyone!" said Mrs. Clark, walking to the front of the classroom. She switched on the projector and connected it to a tablet computer she'd been holding. "Today we'll be watching a short video on creative coding." At the confused looks we gave her, she added, "Using code to express our artistic sides."

The next fifteen minutes were full of amazing images, still and animated, all created on a computer and then displayed on billboards and screens, along with clothing designs, video games, and lights that reacted to music.

Halfway through the video, some kids in the back lost interest and started talking about a new movie coming out. Lucy twisted in her seat and shushed them, earning her some murderous stares and a "Nerd!"

"You're in here, too, you know," I shot back at them.

Lucy gave me a grateful smile and mouthed a thank-you.

At the end of the video, Mrs. Clark turned the lights back on and said, "Ready? Here's your exercise."

We all exchanged puzzled glances, but took out our notebooks.

"I would like you to list as many ways as possible to incorporate coding, both functional *and* creative, into the upcoming school dance." Mrs. Clark pointed to the clock on the wall. "You have three minutes. Go."

My friends and I huddled together.

"I'll jot the ideas down," volunteered Erin, waggling her pencil.

"Okay. Um . . . you could use code to take song requests," said Sophia.

"And to program a robot to greet people," said Leila.

Erin pointed at the screen we'd been watching. "You can program the lights to flicker to the beats of songs."

"You could have light-up squares on the dance floor," I said.

"Or create an app for ticket sales," said Lucy.

"You could program a robot to dance," said Leila.

I shook my head. "We already did that at the hackathon."

"Right. So we know it works," said Leila.

"But that's old. We need new ideas," I said.

Mrs. Clark, who happened to be walking among the groups, stopped at ours. "Let's remember that when we're brainstorming, every idea is valid."

I blushed a little but nodded. "Yes, Mrs. Clark."

Erin added Leila's idea to the list.

"You could program a confetti cannon to go off," said Sophia.

"Ooh, and a balloon drop!" said Erin, writing furiously.

"Shhh. We don't want other groups to hear," Lucy whispered.

We lowered our voices, but when I looked around, the other groups seemed to be finished and just waiting for time to run out.

"Going off Erin's idea, how about bracelets that flash to the beat of the music?" I asked.

"Or a fog machine," said Lucy. She slapped her desk with a hand. "No, a bubble machine!" She definitely wasn't following her own command to keep our voices down.

"And . . . time!" said Mrs. Clark.

Erin lowered her pencil, and we all leaned back in our seats. "Eleven ideas. Not bad!" she said.

Mrs. Clark walked among the groups, collecting idea

sheets. I was pleased to see the other teams had much shorter lists.

"Very impressive," said Mrs. Clark after she'd read each list aloud. "I'm glad *some* of you were paying attention to the video." She gave a pointed look to the kids Lucy had shushed. "But we have a clear winner for sheer volume of ideas." She gestured to me and my friends, and we cheered.

"That's not fair," Bradley spoke up. "We were trying to come up with the best ideas, not a whole list of lame ones."

"Yeah, who wants to go to a dance with a bubble machine?" someone else added.

"Hey, all ideas are valid," I informed them. Out of the corner of my eye, I saw Mrs. Clark smile.

"Maya makes an excellent point," she said. "And now for the special surprise I mentioned. The principal has asked the coding club to design a feature for the dance since we fit the future theme so well—we basically *are* the future." Mrs. Clark turned to my team. "As the winning team, you may choose and control that feature."

My friends and I cheered even louder.

"Seriously unfair," Bradley said. Other kids grumbled their agreement.

"We would've tried harder if we knew the rules and what we were playing for," said Grace.

Mrs. Clark remained impassive. "There was only one rule: write as many ideas as you can. And it shouldn't matter what you're playing for. You should always want to do your best work."

"If you guys want, you can help with whatever we choose for the dance," Lucy offered.

"Yeah, someone might need to fill up the bubble machine," said Erin with a teasing grin.

Later, when my friends and I were leaving coding club, Leila asked, "Um . . . we're not *really* doing the bubble machine, are we?" She put her hand on Lucy's arm. "No offense."

Lucy waved her off. "Please. If we're going to be featured at a futuristic dance, I don't want to be remembered for a bubble machine."

"But that brings up a good question," said Erin. "What *should* we do?"

The five of us walked in thoughtful silence until I cleared my throat.

"Not to sound biased, but I like my light-up bracelet idea," I said. "At first everyone will think they're wearing cheesy plastic bracelets. Then suddenly the beat drops." I pointed to an imaginary bracelet on my wrist. "And the party begins."

My friends laughed.

"How many people are going to this dance?" asked Sophia.

Since I was on the dance committee, I knew the exact count. "A hundred and three."

Sophia shook her head. "Sorry, Maya, but there's no way the school will pay for that many sound-reactive bracelets."

"We could add the cost of the bracelet to the price of the dance ticket," I suggested.

"The dance is a week away," pointed out Leila. "Most people have already bought their tickets."

"Which throws out my ticket app idea," said Lucy.

We settled on the floor by the front entrance of school to watch for our parents' cars.

"Okay, so, no bubble machine, no light-up bracelets, and no ticket app," said Erin. She pulled out the list and a pencil, scratching through ideas.

"What are our other options?" asked Sophia.

Erin read them off, crossing out fog machine, confetti machine, and balloon drop for not being, in her words, "epic" enough.

"Since this dance is in the gym, I think we also have to get rid of the light-up-dance-floor idea," said Lucy. "That space is so big, it'll cost way too much."

Leila sighed. "And if we're looking to make a big impact, I'll give up my robot ideas, too."

Erin held up her list. "That leaves taking song requests or setting up the lights to react to music."

"With bracelets to match," I said quickly.

My friends groaned and protested.

"They would make great souvenirs!" I tried again.

"I vote for lights," said Erin, holding up a hand.

"Lights," said Leila, holding up her hand, too. So did Lucy and Sophia.

All four looked at me.

"If you're not getting the bracelets, this is the next best thing," Leila pointed out.

"Fine," I muttered, raising my hand.

"Great!" Erin circled it on the list. "We'll let Mrs. Clark know tomorrow. I'll bet she can get us permission to meet in the library during homeroom."

"My ride's here." Sophia got to her feet. "See you guys tomorrow!"

I glanced out the front door and saw her parents' minivan pull up, along with Leila's dad's car.

"I'm out, too. Later!" she said.

One by one my friends left, but my stepdad didn't show. I was about to text him when Lucy poked her head in from the front door and said, "Maya, there are some ladies here to pick you up."

"Ladies?" I repeated, getting to my feet.

I didn't recognize the car outside, but then the rear passenger window rolled down, and Nicole's face appeared.

"Maya! We're taking you home today!" she shouted.

I waved goodbye to Lucy and approached the car slowly. I'd never met Nicole's parents, so I didn't know what to expect. But when the front passenger window rolled down, it was Nicole's aunt Liz who smiled up at me.

"Hey, Maya! Great to see you!"

Liz's girlfriend, Ash, leaned over from the driver's side.

"Hi, stranger!"

"Hi!" I smiled at them and climbed into the back seat next to Nicole. "Nicole, I figured you'd be with your parents."

She shook her head. "They're still finalizing things at our old house, so I'm staying with my aunts for now." She bounced excitedly in her seat. "Oh! And your stepdad said you could come over for dinner, which is why we picked you up."

"If I remember, you like pizza," said Liz, glancing over her shoulder at me.

"Who doesn't?" I replied with a grin.

"Nicole tells us you're in a coding club," said Ash, pulling the car away from the curb. "That sounds fun."

"It is," I said. "And my group won a contest in our meeting today, so we get to program the lights for the school dance. We're going to have them pulse to the music."

"Awesome!" said Liz, reaching back for a high five.

I slapped her palm. "I thought we could take it further and give everyone a *bracelet* that pulses to the music."

"Oh my gosh, yes! Do that!" said Nicole, nodding so hard, her earrings swung back and forth.

I shook my head. "The other girls voted against it."

"Pfft. They're crazy," Nicole scoffed. "Your idea sounds way better. Bracelets would be like souvenirs from the dance."

I threw my hands in the air. "That's exactly what I said!"

"Genius is never appreciated in its own time," said Ash.

Nicole clucked her tongue. "Yeah, your friends don't appreciate you!"

I thought for a moment. "They really don't." I sighed deeply and leaned back in the seat.

Nicole bumped me. "You know what might make you feel better? Face squash."

Ash and Liz chuckled from the front, and I tilted my head.

"What's face squash?" I asked.

"It's exactly like it sounds," said Liz.

Nicole grinned. "My aunts came up with it. They have a copy machine, so you press your cheek against the glass, close your eyes, and make a copy of your squashed face. The image is hilarious." She pulled out her phone and showed me some of the images she'd saved.

I couldn't help laughing. "Sure, why not?"

So while Ash and Liz ordered pizza, Nicole and I hung out in their home office, photocopying our faces in all sorts of weird expressions. When we shared our photocopies with Liz and Ash at dinner, they laughed, too.

"I love these the most." Liz held up two papers.

"Those poses were Maya's idea," said Nicole. "She always comes up with the best stuff."

I blushed and grabbed a piece of pizza. "Yours were good, too!"

"Yeah, but adding the little 'Help me!' speech bubble? That was genius."

Liz and Ash carried their plates to the dining room, and Nicole and I followed.

"You know what would be so funny?" she said. "If we taped those pictures on the bulletin boards at school."

I giggled. "Or if we taped them in classroom windows,

like we're actually smashed against the glass."

Nicole squealed with laughter. "Dude, you are so clever."

"Thanks," I said, smiling at her with newfound admiration.

She was right. I *was* clever.

So why couldn't my friends from coding club see it?

Chapter Four

Parents always seem to know when you're having too much fun. They also know the sentence that can stop it: Time to come home.

That was the text I got from Mom while Nicole and I were in her kitchen, eating ice cream.

I lowered my spoon with a sigh. "Nicole, I have to go."

"Now?" She asked around a mouthful of Rocky Road. "But we were gonna read *Teen Vogue* and get disappointed about the clothes we can't afford."

"Some other time," I said. "Can one of your aunts take me home?"

My house was only a few blocks away, but I'd seen enough TV crime dramas to know not to walk alone after dark.

"Sure," Liz said when Nicole asked. "I can take you." She reached for my ice cream bowl, and I handed it over.

"Thanks," I said. "For everything."

"Of course! We're always happy to see you," said Liz.

The sentiment was not the same at my house.

When I walked through our front door, Mom was leaning against the entry wall, arms crossed. I jumped when I saw her.

"Jeez!" I put a hand over my pounding heart. "Have you been standing there since you texted me?"

"Oliver says Liz Davis picked you up from school today," Mom said by way of response. "And that you were hanging out with her niece, Nicole."

Uh-oh.

"Um . . . I was," I said, pulling off my boots.

"Please tell me Liz has two nieces named Nicole," said Mom. "And this isn't the girl you got into trouble with last summer."

"No, it's the same one. But she's changed." I picked up my boots and headed toward my bedroom.

"Changed . . . from shoplifting to grand theft auto?" asked Mom, following me down the hall. "Does she want you to be part of her street crew?"

I gazed up at the ceiling before turning to respond. "First of all, I'm only thirteen. No gang will take me in yet."

Mom opened her mouth, but when she realized I

was joking, she clamped it shut.

"Second, Nicole changed in a good way," I said. "She apologized."

"Ohhh. She apologized." Mom pretended to wipe sweat off her forehead. "I feel better."

"You should! I do."

"Because you're young and naïve." Mom held my face in her hands. "Sweetheart, this girl will do anything to get back into your good graces. She misses having a partner in crime."

I backed out of Mom's hands. "She does not."

"Really?" Mom crossed her arms again. "Did she start apologizing as soon as she saw you?"

"No, ha!" I said smugly. "She hugged me first."

Mom smirked. "But she did apologize pretty quickly. Has she given you any gifts? Maybe something she knows you love?"

"Pfft. No!" I said.

Gum didn't count as a gift, did it?

"She will," said Mom.

"Whatever," I replied. "You don't know what you're talking about."

I walked through the living room, and Mom followed.

"I don't want you spending time with her, Maya. She's trouble."

I spun to face her. "What if she is?" I put my hands on my hips. "You think I'll go along with whatever she says?"

"You did this summer," Mom argued.

"I didn't know better. I do now!"

Oliver emerged from his study. "It's getting a little loud out here. Everything okay?"

"No. Tell her to stay out of my business." I glared at Mom, who set her jaw.

"And tell *her* to listen to reason," said Mom.

Oliver looked from Mom to me. "I feel like you're standing close enough to have heard each other."

Mom pointed at me. "I forbid you to spend time with Nicole."

"Whoa, whoa, whoa." Oliver waved his arms. "Let's not lay down ultimatums just yet."

The fiery look he got from Mom should've burned off his eyebrows.

"If Nicole says she's changed, shouldn't we wait for her to do wrong before we mistrust her?" asked Oliver.

"That's terrible logic," said Mom. "Do you wait for a hurricane to hit before you decide it could do any damage?"

Oliver frowned. "I think you might be overreacting."

Mom's eyes widened, and she turned to face him. That was my cue to escape.

"Overreacting?" I heard her say. "Did you forget—"

I closed my bedroom door and heaved a sigh of relief. I knew Mom wasn't a Nicole fan, but I didn't realize she disliked her *this* much.

I pulled out my phone to text Nicole and saw that I'd missed a string of texts from Erin. The first one started off pretty normal.

By the seventh one, she'd gotten a little frantic.

And that text came three minutes after the first.

I dialed her number, and she picked up right away.

"Oh, thank God! I thought you were mad at me, too!"

"Uh…hello. And no, I was being yelled at by my mother," I said. "Why would I be mad at you, too?" I paused. "Who else is mad?"

"Well, Sophia got snippy when I asked her what she was wearing to the dance," said Erin. "Then Lucy barked at me when I was complaining about what to wear to the dance.

And then *you* got mad when you didn't get your way with the light-up bracelets."

I bristled at her choice of words. "I wasn't mad because I didn't 'get my way.' I'm not a spoiled brat."

"Of course you're not!" Erin was quick to agree. "Man, I am really bad with words today."

"It's fine," I said, sitting on the floor. "I was just upset because nobody considered my ideas."

"I did," she said. "But Sophia's right. Those bracelets would be expensive, and we don't have a big budget. This is a school dance with punch from the cafeteria that's been watered down to serve more people."

I smiled. "That's incredibly specific."

"I've been to a lot of school dances," Erin informed me. "And spent a lot of time around the punch bowl."

"Aw." I tilted my head to one side. "Because nobody wanted to dance with you?" I teased.

I could practically hear Erin rolling her eyes at me. "No, because punch is awesome."

I snickered. "Glad to know you go for the right reasons."

"Yep. Watered-down punch and off-brand potato chips."

We both laughed. But again, since parents can tell when you're having too much fun, Mom poked her head in.

"Who are you talking to?" she demanded.

I cupped a hand over my phone. "Erin."

Mom smiled. "Oh, good. Tell her I said hi! And when you get off the phone, we need to talk."

She waited for me to nod before she closed the door. In a softer voice, I told Erin, "You and I are never ending this phone call."

"Why is your mom mad?" Erin asked.

I told her about Mom's disapproval of Nicole, but when I came to the part where Mom and I started fighting, Erin groaned. "You really want to play that game?"

I wrinkled my forehead. "What game?"

"Defy the Parent."

"If my mom is being unfair, yes," I said. "You don't think I should?"

Erin hesitated. "It would be one thing if your mom said 'Get off the phone! No friends!' But she seems to be singling out Nicole."

"Exactly!" I hammered my fist into the carpet. "She's being unfair."

"Or she sees something bad in Nicole that you don't."

I frowned. "You know, I wasn't mad at you, but I can be."

"No, no, no!" said Erin. "I'm not saying I agree with your mom. I'm saying she has her reasons, and I don't think one is 'to be mean to my daughter.'"

What Erin said made a little sense. And I didn't like it.

"Can we talk about something else?" I asked. "Like why Sophia and Lucy might be upset?"

"At me," Erin added.

I shook my head. "I don't think so. When Lucy's mad, she gets really quiet, and when Sophia's mad, she throws things."

"True," said Erin. "So then why did they get so defensive about the dance?"

We both sat for a moment and thought.

I snapped my fingers. "Maybe Sophia's having issues with Sammy."

Erin sucked in her breath. "And maybe Lucy likes him, too! Yes! It fits perfectly."

"We'll talk to them tomorrow before school," I said. "And see if we can help."

"As older and wiser seventh-graders, it's our duty," Erin said. Then in an old lady's voice, she added, "Did I ever tell you kids about the time I went to a school dance that had name-brand potato chips?"

I laughed and attempted my own imitation. "That's right! No Spud Slivers or Taste of 'Tato for us."

Erin let out a squawk of laughter. "Taste of 'Tato!"

Once we'd calmed down, she said, "Thanks for talking

to me, Maya. I feel loads better."

"That's what friends are for," I said. "And really good friends will stay on the phone with you forever so you don't have to talk to your mother."

She snickered. "Sorry, but I've got homework to do. Good luck with your mom!"

"Thanks," I said with a sigh and hung up.

I changed into my most comfortable pajamas and went in search of Mom. She was sitting with Oliver, watching a movie, but paused it when I walked in.

"You wanted to talk?" I asked.

Mom glanced at Oliver, who jumped up.

"I'm going to make some popcorn."

He squeezed my shoulder as he walked past and whispered, "Be nice."

Mom patted the couch cushion next to her, and I sat.

"Why is this friendship with Nicole so important to you?" she asked.

"Because I think people can change." I picked up a pillow and hugged it to me. "And when you don't agree, it makes me feel like you don't think *I've* changed."

The corners of Mom's mouth turned down, and she studied me in silence. For a few moments, the only sound was popcorn bursting from its kernels.

Finally, Mom gave a deep sigh. "If you think Nicole's changed, I suppose I could give her a chance," she said. "I mean, you came home when I asked, so that's a good sign."

"It is," I agreed. After a beat, I ventured to ask, "So can I hang out with Nicole?"

Mom stiffened, but all she said was, "As long as she doesn't get you into trouble."

"She won't," I promised.

After all, it'd only been one day. What kind of mischief could Nicole possibly cause?

The next morning I was running late, so Oliver dropped me off at school. As I approached the entrance, I saw something familiar and horrifying taped inside the windows.

Squashed against the glass were the photocopied faces Nicole and I had made.

"Nooo," I whispered.

I snatched the papers off the windows and crumpled them, hurrying down the hall and stopping outside the library doors, each of which had a window.

Boom. Nicole's face squashed into one.

Boom. Mine squashed into the other.

"Oh, come on!" I exclaimed, ducking into the library.

I ripped the pages off the doors *and* another one of Nicole's face from the librarian's computer screen.

Had Nicole gotten up at sunrise to do this? And how many were there?

Tossing the papers into the trash, I ran back into the hall, almost colliding with Nicole.

"Hey!" she said breathlessly. "I was just coming to put more of these in the library." She held up our faces.

"Don't!" I said, a little too loudly. A group of guys looked at us, and one of them squashed his face with one hand. The others laughed.

Nicole looked confused. "But I thought you said it'd be funny." She gestured to the guys. "*They* think it is."

"Yes, but I didn't want you to actually do it!" I said. "We could get in serious trouble."

"For taping funny pictures in the windows?" she asked with a snort. "How uptight is this school?"

"I don't want to find out." I grabbed the stack of images from her. "How many more did you put up?"

Nicole stared at the ceiling and counted quietly. The higher the number got, the higher my eyebrows rose.

"Twenty," she said. "Well . . . eighteen." She pointed to the now-empty library windows.

"Fifteen, actually," I told her. "I pulled one off a computer screen and two from the school entrance."

"Awww!" She pouted her lower lip. "Those were the best!"

I grabbed her arm. "Nicole, we have to get rid of the others before a teacher sees. Or worse . . . the principal!"

"Ugh. Fine," Nicole said with a dramatic eye roll.

As we walked the halls collecting images, a strange thing happened: Kids begged us to keep the images up and complimented us on our epic prank.

"You almost scared the pants off Mr. Henke!" one girl said, laughing. "He literally screamed when he saw the face in the window."

"So hilarious! Whose idea was it?" someone else asked.

Nicole arched a brow at me, and I couldn't help raising my hand.

"Mine."

A guy high-fived it. "I never knew you were so funny!"

I beamed at him.

Okay, so Nicole should've told me before she put up the pictures, but I'd stopped her before she got us in trouble, so my mom couldn't be upset.

I had everything under control.

As long as my parents never found out.

Chapter Five

One of the best parts of writing code for the school dance was getting to spend homeroom with my friends from coding club. But when I got to the library, nobody seemed to share my enthusiasm.

Leila was playing a game on her phone (we weren't allowed to use our phones in class, but at the library was fine); Erin was sitting in the corner watching Lucy and Sophia; Lucy was staring forlornly at something in her notebook; and Sophia was busy throwing a ball against the wall and ignoring everyone.

"So how's the project for the dance going?" I asked by way of greeting.

"We were waiting for you," said Leila, not looking up from her phone.

Lucy and Sophia *did* look at me but neither said

anything. Sophia threw her ball a little harder.

Only Erin jumped up and approached me. "Where were you this morning? I thought we were going to . . ." She trailed off and subtly angled her head in Lucy and Sophia's direction. "You know."

"Sorry, I was busy talking to some kids who loved the squashed-face prank Nicole and I pulled." I grinned at her. "Did you see?"

"What, those photocopies in the classroom windows?" asked Erin.

I nodded. "Someone said we scared Mr. Henke!"

Leila paused her game. "Really? With a black-and-white, one-dimensional photo? That wasn't scary."

"I know," I said, walking over to her. "But you've got to admit, it was pretty funny."

"I guess," she said with a shrug.

I looked at Erin for confirmation, and she tilted her hand from side to side. "Putting them in all the windows was overkill."

I flicked my hair to the side. "Well, a lot of other people found it funny."

"Maybe someone bullied them into saying that," said Sophia.

I exchanged a puzzled look with Erin.

"What?" I asked.

"Your little buddy," said Sophia, clearing absolutely nothing up.

"I don't—"

"Do I need to spell it out for you? N-I-C-O-L-E." Sophia punctuated each letter with the bounce of the ball.

I reached out and caught it. "What are you talking about?"

Sophia rocked her chair onto its back legs. "This morning she tried to bully me and Lucy into agreeing with your light-up bracelet idea."

I stepped back. "She what?"

"Nicole didn't bully us, Sophia," Lucy finally spoke up. "It's not like she threatened to hurt us or called us names."

Sophia held up a finger. "I believe she said 'you guys are idiots if you don't use Maya's idea,' and last time I checked, 'idiot' was a name."

I put Sophia's ball on the table and pressed my hands to my cheeks, which were hot with embarrassment. "I'm so sorry, you guys. I'm sure she was just sticking up for me."

"Maybe she was, but she could've found a nicer way to do it," said Lucy.

"You're right," I said, reaching across the table. "I'll talk to Nicole."

Lucy's expression lightened, and she squeezed my hand. "Thanks."

"Soph?" I reached toward her. She rolled her eyes but offered me a fist to bump.

"We're cool."

"And hey, if you want, I'll have Nicole come apologize," I added.

Sophia grimaced. "No offense, Maya, but I'd rather not breathe the same air as her anytime soon."

Lucy shot her a warning look. "Soph."

"What? I said 'no offense.'"

"Wow." I leaned away from Sophia. "You really don't like Nicole, do you?"

Sophia smiled apologetically. "We saw her hanging those squashed-face pics"—she gestured to herself and Lucy—"and she was cackling like the Wicked Witch of the West."

I looked at Lucy. "Really?"

Lucy squirmed but nodded. "It wasn't a happy laugh. It was more . . . wicked, like she knew she was causing trouble."

No defenses for Nicole came to mind. "Well, at least we didn't *get* in trouble," I said.

"You're lucky," said Leila, who'd resumed her game.

"Last time I put up flyers without permission, I got sent to the principal."

"Yeah, you can't even hang a funny doodle of the math teacher with a chicken body," said Erin.

We all looked at her.

"What? His name's Mr. Cluck. How can I *not* take advantage of that?"

"I'm going to need to see that drawing," said Sophia.

"Oh, sure!" Erin reached for her backpack. "It inspired me to create a whole collection of teachers-as-animals."

I cleared my throat. "Aren't we here to talk about coding for the dance?"

Erin fumbled in her bag with a guilty grin. "I was totally getting my coding notebook, not my teacher-creature one."

"So everyone's getting along now?" asked Leila. "Nobody's mad at anyone?"

"I'm good," I said.

"Me too," said Sophia.

Lucy nodded, and Leila finally put away her game.

"Right. Down to business." Erin uncapped her pen. "We should make a list of parts we need for our project. And before that, we should figure out how to . . . um . . . do our project."

The rest of us laughed.

"First, do we want all the lights to flicker at once?" asked Erin. "Or do we want different colors for different volumes?"

We all agreed different colors would be way more fun.

"The music will come from speakers," added Leila. "So there has to be a way to take that audio signal and transform it into the different-colored lights."

"That's where the code comes in, right?" I asked. "So we need an input: some sort of sensor that picks up the music volume."

Erin did a quick search on her phone. "We can buy an audio sensor that plugs directly into an Arduino circuit board . . . which we'll also need." She started a supply list.

"My sister has a bunch of Arduinos, so we can probably take one," said Leila.

"Cool!" said Erin. "I'll cross that off the list."

"So if the audio sensor's the input, then the flashing of the different-colored lights must be the output," said Sophia.

"And the code to do it all runs on the Arduino," said Erin, taking notes.

"Wait, what are you guys talking about? What's an Arduino? I'm so confused." Lucy buried her head in her hands.

Leila started talking while she drew a human stick figure. "My sister explained this to me recently—she's using an Arduino circuit board for a project of hers. Think of an audio sensor like your ear, and an Arduino circuit board like your brain."

She doodled music notes going from the stick figure's ear to the brain.

"Your brain processes the music that your ear picks up and turns it into something that it understands—"

"Kind of like an Arduino that's running code," said Erin. "Except your brain processes music automatically, while an Arduino has to be *told* to get the input from an audio sensor."

"Exactly!" Leila continued. "Once the Arduino gets the input from the audio sensor, it'll use more code to match the volume level with a light color. The last part of the code sends the information to a relay board that actually controls the lights and tells the different colors to flash."

Now I was the one who was confused. "A relay board?"

Leila drew three little flashlights in the stick figure's hands and labeled them different colors. "Yeah—it's a board with magnetic switches that turn on or off through sensors, and we can write code so that it controls the lights the way we want it to."

Lucy stared at the diagram for a few seconds. "I get it—the hands are turning the lights off and on, so they're like the relay board!" She leaned back with a satisfied smile.

"You are seriously good at explaining this stuff," I told Leila, studying her diagram.

She grinned. "It helps to have a sister who's even more into robotics than I am."

"So if we want three colors, we need to run three connections off the Arduino," said Erin.

"And add extra code for each color, right?" asked Sophia.

"Yeah, but it's just making minor tweaks to each line depending on the light color," Leila answered. "So we can just copy, paste, edit."

I was amazed that we were figuring all this out so quickly. I guess we'd learned a lot in a few months of coding club—and of course it helped that Leila and Erin already knew some coding stuff.

"And there are five of us," I pointed out, "so we can divide and conquer."

Erin looked at the list she had created. "Leila, I think it's probably easiest for you to come up with parts."

She gave a thumbs-up. "On it."

Erin smiled. "Great! Who wants to write the code that makes the Arduino look for the audio sensor?"

I raised my hand. "Me!"

"And I'll write the code to turn the music into light colors," said Erin, making a note.

"I can help, and maybe Mrs. Clark can, too," Leila told her. "That section might get tricky. It takes a *lot* of figuring out."

Erin nodded. "So, Lucy and Sophia, can you write the output code to send the light colors to the relay board?"

Sophia nodded, and so did Lucy, but she was twirling her pen nervously between her fingers.

"We can all work together," Leila assured her. "Why don't we meet at my house after school and get started?"

The rest of us agreed. I had a feeling Mom would be happy I was spending time with anyone but Nicole.

"I'll run our final plan past Mrs. Clark," said Erin. "As long as she's okay with our setup, we're good to go."

The bell rang for the end of homeroom, and we gathered our things. I waited for Erin, and we walked to our lockers.

"So I know how Sophia and Lucy feel. Do you dislike Nicole, too?" I asked.

Erin pressed her lips together and squinted thoughtfully. "I don't know her well enough to dislike her," she said. "But I don't think she's changed as much as she says."

"You'd be surprised. She's pretty sweet," I said, opening

my locker. Taped inside the door was a photocopied image of Nicole's squashed face.

"Surprise!" Nicole appeared beside me, and I yelped. "I saved you one as a souvenir."

Erin smirked at me. "Pretty sweet, indeed. Later!"

Before I could respond, she disappeared into the crowd.

"So do you like it?" Nicole tapped the picture.

"I guess," I said, frowning. "How did you get in my locker?"

Nicole leaned closer. "I'm an office aide during homeroom. You want a locker combo? I can get it," she said with a wink.

"Thanks, I'm all set," I said. "But next time, please ask before you open my locker, okay?"

Nicole bit her lip. "You're mad, aren't you? Shoot! I thought you'd like your surprise."

"I do," I said, "but I also like my personal space."

Nicole's expression turned serious. "I completely understand. It won't happen again."

She reached into her purse and pulled out two pieces of gum. "Want one?"

I thought about what my mom had said about presents. "Sure," I finally said, taking a stick. "And while we're talking personal space, I heard you told my coding club friends to agree with my light-up bracelet idea."

Nicole stopped mid chew. "Was that wrong, too?"

"It wasn't *wrong*. I know you meant well, but it made them mad at me."

Nicole gripped my hand. "Oh no! I'm so sorry!"

"That's okay," I said. "But it might be best if you leave the coding club alone. It's really important to me, and if I'm going to make anybody mad, I'd rather do it myself." I finished with a teasing smile.

Nicole relaxed and smiled back. "Of course. Coding club and your locker are off-limits!" She crossed her heart with a fingertip.

I breathed a sigh of relief. "Thanks." I grabbed my books and shut my locker. "I didn't tell you this morning, but I love that top, by the way!" I nodded to her blouse: green with silver accents on the sleeves and collar.

"Oh, thanks!" said Nicole. She told me about a sale where she'd bought it, and I couldn't help marveling at how much she really had changed. The new Nicole was super apologetic when she screwed up, didn't get defensive, and paid for things.

My friends had her all wrong.

Chapter Six

"We have a small problem," Erin said, when I got to Leila's that afternoon.

"We're out of onion ring chips!" piped up Leila from her kitchen.

"We have two small problems," Erin amended, with a sigh. She shouted over her shoulder. "What about onion soup mix?"

Leila poked her head into the living room where Erin and I were sitting with Lucy and Sophia. "You want to eat a packet of soup mix?"

"Don't be ridiculous," Erin said with a snort. "I want to pour it over popcorn."

Leila stared at her. "Sure. Because that's less disgusting."

"What's the other small problem?" I asked Erin while Leila disappeared back into her kitchen.

"Mrs. Clark said we can't use the gym's light system," said Erin. "In case something goes wrong, the school doesn't want us to fry their ten-thousand-dollar set of bulbs."

"Yikes," I said. "But that makes sense. What do we do now?"

"Come up with another solution," said Sophia. "Like a different light source."

My heart skipped a beat. If they were looking for a different light source—

"You know . . . ," I said in my most casual voice. "There's still my bracelet idea."

Everyone groaned, including Leila from the other room.

"Maya, no! We already said that idea was too expensive," said Sophia.

"We'll have people pay for them before we buy the supplies," I insisted. "Wouldn't you buy one?"

Sophia got quiet, so I turned to Lucy. "I know you want to get a special guy's attention," I said with a conspiratorial wink. Lucy blushed. "With a light-up bracelet, he'll be watching you all—"

"Christmas!" exclaimed Erin.

I blinked in surprise. "I was going to say 'night.'"

Erin shook her head so hard her glasses slipped. "I was

trying to think of other lights we could program, and then it hit me."

Sophia's eyes brightened, and she pointed at Erin. "Christmas lights! We can program them to music!"

"I thought the theme of the dance was the future," said Leila. She walked in with a bowl of popcorn, cups, and a packet of onion soup mix. "Won't Christmas lights just feel . . . festive?"

"They sell strands in single colors," said Erin, scooping popcorn into a cup. "We could get blue ones and white ones . . ." She handed the popcorn to Lucy, who almost flung it everywhere in her excitement.

"Oh! And orange and gray ones, like our school colors!" she exclaimed.

"That could work." Leila nodded.

Clearly, my bracelet idea wasn't going anywhere.

"Erin, do you think we can pull it off?" I asked.

She handed me a cup of popcorn and nodded. "We'll still need some sort of relay board we can plug into the wall since there's no way the Arduino can power that many lights by itself. But after that, we just have to plug a bunch of light strings together, connect them to the relay board, and connect *that* to the Arduino."

Once everyone had their popcorn, Erin ripped open the

packet of onion soup mix and sprinkled it over hers. She moved to toss the rest of the packet back onto the tray, but Leila stopped her.

"Oh no. You wanted a packet, you have to eat a packet," Leila said with a mischievous grin.

Erin shrugged and poured the rest of the onion soup mix into her mouth.

The rest of us freaked out.

"Ewww!" said Lucy.

"Gross gross gross!" Leila scooted away from Erin.

Erin burped and fanned the air in front of her face. "I might regret that for the rest of the day."

Caught in the blast zone, I pinched my nose. "Try the rest of the week."

"It smells like a wet cat in gym socks threw up a little," added Sophia.

Erin just hummed and ate her popcorn.

"To get back to our project," said Leila, "how many sets of lights do you think we need?"

"That depends on where we want to hang them," I said. "Are we putting them around the door frames or around the refreshment table?"

Erin's eyes lit up at the word *refreshment*, and she grinned at me. I smiled but put a finger to my lips.

"We could string the lights on the wall between the two," said Lucy. "Kind of like we saw in that coding club video."

"Good idea!" said Erin. "That way, people dancing can enjoy it, and so can people hanging by the refreshment table." She coughed into her hand, but it suspiciously sounded like, "Me!"

Leila and I laughed. Sophia and Lucy did not.

"Jeremiah asks you to the dance, and all you want to do is drink punch and stand around?" Lucy asked incredulously.

Erin blinked in confusion. "Well, yeah. If I drink punch and dance, I get a stomachache."

Lucy crossed her arms. "If *I* were going with someone, I would not treat them like that."

And then I realized Lucy's crush was on *Erin's* date, not Sophia's.

Unfortunately, Erin hadn't figured this out.

Erin turned to Sophia and said, "Look, you clearly don't want to go to the dance with Sammy, and Lucy does. Why not let her?"

"Huh?" Sophia said.

"What?" Lucy said.

"Uh ... Erin?" I said.

Erin held up a hand to silence me. "Sophia, you don't

have to cover it up anymore. I know that's why you've been so mopey when we bring up the dance. You hate your date."

"Ohhh," said Leila.

Sophia turned pink. "That's not true!"

Erin patted her leg. "Shh. It's okay. But at least set him free so Lucy can have him."

Lucy let out an indignant squeak. "I don't want Sammy! I want Jeremiah!" As soon as she said the words, she clapped a hand over her mouth.

"Whoa!" Leila watched them and nibbled her popcorn. "You guys are better than Netflix."

Erin ignored her and turned to Lucy. "You wanted to go to the dance with *my* date?"

Lucy ducked her head but nodded. "I was going to ask him the day he asked you."

"Oh." Erin bit her lip. "I feel bad now. I'll tell him I can't go."

Lucy's eyes widened. "No! Don't do that just for me. If you like him, you should go." She paused and tentatively asked, "*Do* you like him?"

"Well, yeah, but I don't want you to be sad."

"And I don't want *you* to be sad." Lucy poked her. "But I also don't want you to take Jeremiah for granted."

Erin smiled. "Would you feel better if I told you Jeremiah was the one who suggested hanging out at the refreshment table? He hates to dance."

Lucy frowned. "He does?"

"Mm-hm. Almost as much as he hates cats."

"What?" Lucy clutched a hand to her heart. "But cats are the best!"

"I know." Erin shrugged. "I couldn't even get him to like kittens."

At that, we all made sounds of protest.

"Okay, *nobody* should go to the dance with him," declared Leila. "If he can't fall in love with teeny tiny paws, he's dead inside."

Lucy studied Erin for a moment. "You know what? Have fun with Jeremiah."

Erin raised an eyebrow. "Are you sure?"

Lucy nodded. "I'm starting to realize I didn't know him like I thought I did."

Leila brushed her hands together. "That takes care of that!"

I held up a finger. "Wait a minute. We figured out why Lucy was upset, but I thought it had to do with why Sophia was upset."

"Me too," said Erin.

She, Leila, Lucy, and I looked at Sophia, who shrugged.

"I was bummed for Lucy," she said.

"You were? That's so sweet!" Lucy pounced on Sophia with a hug.

Sophia laughed and patted her arm. "I just want you to be happy."

"Hey, since neither of us has to meet someone before the dance," I said, getting Lucy's attention, "come over early, and I'll give us both makeovers."

Lucy's face lit up. "Cool! I'm in!"

"Well, I still need to buy something to wear," said Erin. "If anyone wants to go shopping, my mom is taking me after this."

"I'll go with you, but I've already got my outfit," I said. I pulled up the picture of my dress on my phone.

My friends *ooh*ed and *ahh*ed.

"I'm going to wear a superhero costume," said Leila. "Because that's what I'd like to see in the future."

Erin smiled. "Nice! So do you want to go shopping and . . . pick up a golden lasso or whatever?"

Leila laughed. "I'm not going as Wonder Woman. I'm going as Ms. Marvel. She's, like, the only Pakistani American superhero." Leila showed us a picture on *her* phone.

"Awesome," said Sophia.

"So cool!" I said.

"Okay, no lasso, then," Erin told Leila. "Do you want to go pick up your giant lightning bolt instead?"

The rest of us laughed.

"I wish I could," said Leila. "But my parents want to go out tonight, so I have to babysit my little brother."

Erin turned to Lucy. "How about it? Wanna go shopping with me and Maya?"

"Sure! Sophia, you want to come?"

Sophia waved her away. "Nah, I've got sports stuff to do," she said. "But send pictures of what you get." Sophia's voice sounded a lot lighter than the expression on her face looked.

"Of course!" said Erin. "For now, though, we should probably get to work on this project."

While we searched the Internet for coding help, Lucy, Leila, and I whispered about the dance. Occasionally, Erin would jump in with a comment, and almost everyone would laugh. The only one who stayed quiet was Sophia.

A half hour later, we had a rough idea of what we were doing but knew we'd still need help with some of the trickier technical parts. Luckily, Leila was confident her coding-savvy sister could step in.

While my friends talked, I texted my mom to make sure I could go to the mall with Erin and Lucy. Since I hadn't mentioned Nicole, Mom gave her approval *and* a smiley face emoji. I was about to respond when a text came in from Nicole.

 wanna hang out?? 😊 😊 😊

Erin clapped her hands. "Great work, everyone! Time to shut it down and go shopping!"

"Woo-hoo!" Lucy cheered. When I didn't, she raised one of my arms for me. "Woo-hoo!"

"Um . . . can Nicole come with us?" I asked.

Lucy promptly dropped my arm. "Boo-hoo."

Erin made a pained expression. "Does she *have* to?"

I frowned. "She doesn't *have* to, but it would be nice for her to make more friends."

"So let her decide that," said Sophia from where she was packing her bag. "She hasn't tried to get to know any of us. Why should we make the extra effort?"

"That's not tr—nice," I said. She was kind of right. Nicole didn't seem to spend time with anyone but me.

"Fine," I said, texting Nicole back. As I typed, I said the message aloud. "Sorry, can't. Have plans."

"Thanks," said Lucy. "Maybe we can all hang out some other time, but I just want it to be our group today. And Nicole's . . . you know."

She didn't have to say it, but I could fill in the blanks. *Nicole's an outsider.*

"Sure," I said.

Lucy got to her feet. "For now, we have places to be and things to buy!"

"Shoppinggg!" Erin sang, hoisting her backpack onto her shoulder. "Let's go!" She pulled me to a standing position.

"Woo-hoo!" Lucy cheered again.

"Have fun!" Leila told us.

"How can we not?" I said, forcing a lighthearted laugh.

Since I *was* excited about shopping and I'd argued with my friends enough for one day, I decided to let it go.

There was no way they were making me the next outsider.

Chapter Seven

"Are we ready for fun?" Erin's mom asked when she picked us up.

"Yep!" Lucy said.

"Yep!" Erin said.

"Nope," I said, looking around me. "I forgot my scarf. Be right back!"

I hopped out of the car and ran to Leila's front door.

"Leila," I said, throwing it open, "I—"

She and Sophia both glanced up in surprise. They were sitting on the couch, and Leila had a comforting arm around Sophia, who had her elbows on her knees and a scowl on her face.

"Hey, what's wrong?" I stepped inside, closing the door behind me.

"I thought you were going to the mall with Erin and

Lucy," Sophia said. She'd stopped scowling, but her forehead was still wrinkled.

"I am, but I forgot my scarf." I grabbed it off the couch. "Are you okay?"

"Yeah. Great," said Sophia in a voice that sounded the opposite.

I sat on her other side. "Why don't I believe that?"

"It's just...I'm a little..." Sophia pressed her lips together.

"Teapot?" I ventured. Leila stifled a giggle, and Sophia finally cracked a smile.

"No," she said. "I'm a little bummed that you guys are talking about new dresses for the dance. I . . . I can't really afford one."

"That's okay." I waved away Sophia's concern. "Wear one you already have."

Sophia snorted. "I only *have* one."

My mouth fell open. "What?"

Sophia nodded. "Money's pretty tight for my family, so dresses aren't exactly a top priority."

"Ohhh." I knew she had a lot of sisters and getting a babysitter for them was often an issue because of money, but I hadn't thought about whether or not she could buy new clothes—especially since she was usually in her sports gear, anyway.

"She didn't want to say anything because she was embarrassed," added Leila.

I shifted to face Sophia completely. "You know we won't judge you for wearing that dress. You can even borrow one of mine, if you want."

Sophia shook her head, cheeks reddening. "This is my first dance with a guy. I wanted the dress to be mine, and I wanted it to be special."

I slumped on the couch. Outside, a car horn honked, and I knew it was Erin's mom, but I wasn't in a hurry to go to the mall anymore.

"Sophia, I'm so sorry," I said. "If we'd known—"

She waved my apology away. "It's okay. And I'm sorry I didn't support your light-up bracelet idea. It *is* cool, but when you said people had to buy them, it was just one more thing I knew I couldn't afford."

My hands went up to my mouth. "The light-up bracelet," I whispered. Then in a slightly louder voice, "The light-up bracelet!"

"Yeah," she said, giving me a curious look.

You know how great ideas are described as a lightbulb clicking on over someone's head? For me, it was as if someone lit a fire under me.

"That's it!" I leaped from the couch and spun to face my

startled friends. "Sophia, we could make your dress light up!"

She gave me a puzzled look. "Huh?"

With a gasp, Leila jumped up, too. "We totally could! It's perfect!"

She and I squealed and hugged each other, but Sophia stayed where she was.

"Could one of you please explain?" she asked in a loud voice.

I pulled away from Leila. "We'll take the same stuff we're using for the lights at the dance," I explained, "and we'll make your dress light up to the music."

"I bet my sister even has all the materials, so we won't have to buy anything," Leila said.

I high-fived her. "Perfect!"

Sophia rose slowly from the couch, her eyes shining. "Can you really do that?"

"You'll have to wear a small battery pack," said Leila, grinning. "But yes."

I gestured to Sophia. "Sophia Torres, on Saturday, you are going to sparkle—literally."

Finally, Sophia joined in our excitement. With a shriek, she launched herself at us, and we caught her, laughing.

"Thank you, thank you, thank you!" she exclaimed, jumping up and down.

Leila and I joined in.

The three of us were so busy hopping around and hollering that we didn't realize Lucy had come back inside, until she was hopping along with us.

"Is this what's been taking so long?" she asked. "Also, why are we doing it?"

"I'm getting a light-up dress for the dance!" crowed Sophia.

"Awesome!" Lucy cheered. "Not to spoil the moment, but Maya, we have to go!"

"Right!" I said, bouncing toward the door.

Lucy giggled and bounced after me.

"See you guys tomorrow!" I waved to Leila and Sophia.

Lucy opened the door, and we hurried down the steps to Erin's mom's car.

"What took so long?" asked Erin when we got in.

"Sorry," I said, buckling my seat belt. "Leila, Sophia, and I were talking."

"And bouncing," added Lucy.

"Aww, I missed bouncing?" Erin asked.

"The mall has a trampoline store if you're that torn up," said her mom, pulling away from the curb.

Lucy leaned forward. "Erin just ate a ton of onion soup mix on her popcorn. You may not want that coming back up."

Erin's mom wrinkled her nose at her daughter. "Onion mix with popcorn?"

"Thank you!" I said.

"It was yummy," said Erin. "And I'm going to suggest they serve it at the dance."

"Well, at least that'll keep anyone from wanting to kiss you," her mom mused.

Lucy and I laughed, and Erin buried her face in her hands.

"Mom, you're not supposed to talk about that stuff!" she said in a muffled voice.

Her mom leaned toward Erin and started making smooching sounds. "Oh, Jeremiah, you're *so* dreamy!"

"Dreamy? Nobody says that, Mom," Erin informed her.

I glanced at Lucy for a reaction to Jeremiah's name, but she was giggling at the conversation between Erin and her mom.

I settled back in my seat and smiled.

Lucy was happy, Leila was happy, Erin was happy, and now, thanks to me, Sophia was happy. Plus, I was getting to use a form of my light-up bracelet idea, and that made *me* happy. Not bad for an afternoon of coding!

The next morning when I walked into school with Erin, Nicole was waiting for me.

"Good morning!" she greeted us. "Maya, can I talk to you alone?"

I glanced at Erin, and she waved to us both.

"Catch up with you in homeroom!" she told me.

As Erin disappeared into the hall traffic, I faced Nicole. "What's going on? Is everything okay?"

"Oh yeah!" Nicole gave an airy laugh. "Sorry, I didn't mean to sound serious. I just thought I'd make plans with you for tonight before anyone else could."

I sucked in my breath. "Actually I do have plans. I'm meeting some of the girls from coding club—"

"Again?" Nicole's eyes widened. "You have to meet them after school, then during homeroom, then at lunch, and then in the evening . . ."

"It's a lot," I agreed. I'd actually had to let go of my dance-committee duties to make it happen. "But I don't mind. And tonight's meeting was my choice."

"Your choice?" She narrowed her eyes. "As in, normally they make you go?"

I laughed and nudged her to start walking with me. "They don't make me do anything. It's not like that."

"Sounds that way to me." Nicole tugged my backpack strap so I'd stop walking. "Maya, they're treating you like you don't matter. You need to put yourself first."

"I will once the dance is over," I said. "For now, I need to do what's best for the team."

The hackathon had definitely shown me how much smoother things went when everyone worked toward the same goal.

Nicole parked a hand on her hip. "Fine. Then how about tomorrow after school? Are you free for an hour or two?"

I thought for a moment. "Tomorrow should work," I said.

"I'm putting it on my calendar," Nicole said, pulling out her phone.

"And I'm heading to the library," I told her.

"Okay." She glanced up from her phone. "But remember that your feelings matter, and they should appreciate you."

I grinned at her. "Yes, Mom."

Nicole went back to typing. "I like your mother. I'll take that as a compliment."

If only my mom felt the same way about her.

When the bell rang to start homeroom, my friends from coding club and I were waiting for Mrs. Clark, who wanted to check on our progress.

"We came up with a backup plan since we couldn't use the school lights," Erin told her. "We've decided to do a light display on one of the gym walls."

"Creative coding," said Mrs. Clark with a nod of approval.

"Do you have all the components you need?"

"I took some measurements of the gym this morning," Leila told her. She handed Mrs. Clark a sheet of paper. "I've written down the number of light strings we'll need and the colors. All together, the lights shouldn't cost more than fifty dollars. I also wrote down an audio sensor and relay board that we need."

Mrs. Clark glanced at the note. "You know that I, or another adult, will have to handle any electrical wiring." She looked around at us all, and we nodded. Satisfied, she pocketed Leila's paper. "Then I don't think any of that should be a problem. How's the code coming?"

I was about to tell her I'd been researching how to get the Arduino to find the sensor input when Erin said, "We're done with the sensor input. Now we're working on the next step."

I shot her a quick glance. "We are? Because I'm working on it, and that's news to me."

"Uh-oh," Lucy said under her breath.

Mrs. Clark rubbed her chin. "Are we not communicating, ladies?"

Erin sucked air through her teeth. "Maya, I meant to tell you on the bus. My dad called last night and talked me through some of the coding stuff. The first part was pretty easy, so I went ahead and wrote it."

"You what?" This was exactly what Nicole had been talking about. Erin was treating me like I didn't matter. "But that was *my* part. Why didn't you just work on your own stuff?"

The words came out a little sharper than I intended, and Erin slid back in her chair.

"Sorry, I thought you'd be cool with it since you're busy with other projects." Erin glanced in Sophia's direction. "Clearly I was wrong."

"It's fine," I said in a voice that indicated it wasn't. "And I could've done both things."

Erin was turning the color of bubble gum. "I know that. Look, if it's a big deal, you can take the part I was going to work on with Leila."

The process to turn the music into light colors? Wasn't that supposed to be the hardest part?

I jutted out my chin. "Fine. I'm meeting her this afternoon, anyway." I nodded at Leila, who was watching Erin and me with fascination.

Mrs. Clark cleared her throat. "Well, now that we've cleared that up, how about the code to trigger the different lights?"

"I'm getting Sophia to help me with that," said Lucy.

"And Erin, if you have any spare time, I could really use your help, too."

The color in Erin's cheeks lightened a little, and she flashed her best smile at Lucy. "Of course. I'd be happy to help."

Mrs. Clark clapped her hands together. "All right, then. I'd like this by Friday morning so we can do a test run."

I almost fell out of my chair.

"This Friday?" I asked.

Mrs. Clark smiled. "The dance is the following day, so next Friday might be too late."

The other girls giggled.

I forced a smile and nodded. "Of course."

"We can totally do it, no problem!" Leila bumped my shoulder and held up a hand for me to high-five.

Easy for her to say. She hadn't also promised someone a light-up dress. But since I'd made a huge deal about Erin doing my coding, I couldn't admit I was in over my head. So I smacked Leila's hand and said, "Absolutely!"

"I can't wait to see what you ladies come up with," said Mrs. Clark. "And remember, we're all on the same team." Her pointed look landed on Erin and me.

"Yes, Mrs. Clark," said Erin.

"Of course," I said again.

"And have fun with this," Mrs. Clark reminded us all. "It's coding club, for crying out loud!"

We all cheered, but I did feel like crying out loud. If Mrs. Clark wanted to test run the project Friday morning, we'd have to have everything assembled, including the code, by tomorrow night. I really hoped Leila was as good at coding as Erin.

And I hoped I was, too.

Chapter Eight

Erin never apologized.

I kept waiting for her to blurt it out, but all morning she stayed quiet. At lunch I didn't see her because Leila and I ducked into the computer lab and worked on our code. In the afternoon, Erin passed me two different times in the hall and just smiled politely.

I must have looked as annoyed as I felt, because when I got in Mom's car that afternoon, she asked, "Bad day?"

"Erin did my part of the project, and now I have to do a harder part, and she won't apologize, and I do so much for that group, and nobody appreciates me!" I said in one long breath.

Mom blinked at me while I inhaled all the oxygen in the car. "Wow. How long have you been holding *that* in?" she asked.

"Six hours," I told her, buckling my seat belt. "I tried to let a little of it out at lunch, but Leila took Erin's side."

"You bad-mouthed Erin to other people?" asked Mom with wide eyes. "That doesn't sound like you."

"Nicole said I should get it off my chest, and if my friends don't like it, oh well," I told Mom. Nicole had then tricked the snack machine into vending a free bag of M&M's and shared a handful with me. Sadly, it was the best part of my day.

Mom's lips curled. "Now I'm starting to understand." She put the car in gear. "Sweetheart, do you ever think Nicole might be trying to turn you against your friends?"

I shook my head. "No way. She knows they're important to me."

Mom held out a hand. "Which is why she's trying to separate you. She's jealous."

I crossed my arms. "Wrong. When I asked her to stay out of my coding club stuff, she apologized. Apologized! That's more than I can say for Erin."

Mom snorted. "Erin apologizes all the time. When she had dinner with us last week, she apologized twice during the salad course alone."

I threw my hands in the air. "So why won't she apologize for this?"

Mom imitated me. "Because she thinks *you* should!"

"Okay, you are driving. That is not a safe gesture." I pointed to the steering wheel. "And why should I apologize? I didn't ask Erin to write my code."

"No, but she did, anyway, because she's your friend. She just wants a little thanks," said Mom. "Trust me."

"Well, I'll tell her 'thank you' after she apologizes," I muttered.

Mom pulled onto our street. "That might be a long wait, my dear."

"Wanna bet?" I glanced at my phone. No new messages. "Shoot. I was hoping to prove you wrong," I muttered.

Mom chuckled. "When we get home, you can take your mind off things with some homework."

I rolled my eyes. "Very subtle, Mom."

But I only got through a few math problems before the doorbell rang and Sophia appeared.

"Sorry I'm early! I just got so excited," she said when Mom showed her to my room. "And I brought the dress!" She reached into a bag and pulled out a blue dress with a poufy skirt.

I took it from her. "This is perfect! White lights will look great on this."

"You're lighting a dress?" asked Mom. "I thought you

said you were lighting the gym."

"We are, but I'm also doing a side project for Sophia," I told Mom. "Leila's going to bring over the other pieces, and I'm going to sew the lights, Arduino, and battery supply into the dress."

Mom nodded her understanding. "Sophia, are your parents okay with you altering this dress?"

"My mom says I'm outgrowing it, anyway," said Sophia. "And Maya offered to loan me dresses any time I need them, right?" She turned to me, and I gave her a thumbs-up.

"My closet is your shopping mall," I said.

Mom's expression softened, and she kissed the top of my head. "Such a good, smart kid."

"Remember that at allowance time," I said.

Sophia took her dress back from me and held it up. "You're sure you can get this done by Saturday?"

I nodded. "It'll use a code similar to our light display."

"How's the process for music to lights coming?" she asked.

I made a face. "Pretty tough," I admitted. "Leila and I found some usable code online, but when we tried to put in our variables and compile it, we got an error on one of our lines."

"Compile the code?" asked Mom.

"Change it into a language the Arduino can understand," I explained.

"Well, you still have today and tomorrow to figure it out," Sophia reminded me. "And if you're stuck, you can always ask Erin. Thanks to her, we already have the first part done."

I didn't respond until Mom bumped me. "Yes, that was good of her," I said mechanically.

Mom sighed and walked away. "It's a start."

Sophia watched my mom leave. "What was that about?"

"Long story," I said. "Why don't we get to work on your dress?"

She pulled it on over her gym clothes, and I handed her a packet of red dot stickers.

"Let's pretend these are lights," I said. "You have a hundred dots to work with, so arrange them however you want."

Even without actual lights, Sophia glowed as she happily applied the stickers. While she worked, I stepped back and observed.

"Diagonal stripes? I like it!"

"Thanks!" said Sophia. "I thought a pattern would stand out more."

"Spoken like a true fashion designer," I said.

Just as she was finishing up, the doorbell rang again.

"Awesome!" said Leila when she saw our progress. "And it should make wiring the dress easy." She placed a bag on the floor. "Here are the lights and other pieces."

"Great!" I dug through the bag. "Tell your sister I said thanks."

Sophia pounced on the lights and plugged them into the wall. Then she held a section of the shining bulbs up to her dress. "This is going to look so cool." She turned to Leila and me. "Hurry with the code!"

We laughed.

"Are you ready to start?" I asked Leila.

"Yep. And I talked to my sister about the line error we got." Leila removed a notebook from her backpack. "Since that code we found online *was* working, it's got to be something we added that maybe has bad punctuation or spelling or something. And there could be more than one error, since the compiler will usually stop at the first problem."

I made a face. "Great. Well, I guess we should get started and look through our code. Sophia, you want to stay and hang out?"

"I wish I could," she said, "but I have to get home." She

pulled the dress over her head and placed it on my dresser. "Take good care of it."

"I will." I walked her to the front door. "And when I'm done, you won't mind that it's your only dress."

She hugged me. "Thanks again, Maya."

The door closed, and I turned around, almost crashing into Mom.

"Is this your favorite hangout spot?" I asked.

"That's her only dress?" Mom responded.

I put a finger to my lips and pulled Mom down the hall. "Yes, but she doesn't want anyone to know," I whispered. "So never bring it up."

Mom mimed zipping her lips and hugged me. "I'm so proud of you."

"You just zipped your lips. You shouldn't be able to talk," I pointed out but returned the hug.

On the way back to my room, I heard strange music coming through my door. Leila had two applications up on her laptop screen. One was for coding and the other was some sort of video game.

"What are you playing?" I asked as I walked in.

Leila jumped at the sound of my voice and turned around with a guilty expression.

"It's an online game called *Wands and Weapons*," she

said. "And I wasn't playing; I was checking to see if my character had finished mining for gold."

I watched Leila's character inspect a mining cart. "Why?"

"I need the gold to buy a magic dagger to kill the Troll King." Leila clicked on a pile of gold. "Almost there! I just need five more gold pieces." She clicked on a pickax, and her character started hacking away at a cave wall.

Then she minimized the screen and returned to her code.

"What happens when you get five more gold pieces?" I asked.

Leila frowned at her coding screen. "I use the gold to buy an Unwielding Dagger. Then I go under the Bridge of Broken Promises and kill the Troll King. Hopefully."

She crossed off one of the possible syntax errors from the list. "This line's not missing semicolons."

I reached for my own laptop and settled on the floor next to Leila, glancing at my half of the list. "Looks like I'm checking for parentheses."

I found one that was missing, but when I added it, I received an error message for another line. "Shoot! I think we made more than one mistake." I shared my discovery with Leila, who updated her version of the code before pulling up her gaming screen again.

"Finally! Enough gold!" she said, and closed the screen. The flashy graphics and music went away.

"But don't you have to buy the dagger now?" I asked. To be honest, I kind of wanted to see more of the game.

"Oh, I can do that after we debug this code," said Leila. "But first we have to find what else is wrong and fix it. This line doesn't need semicolons or parentheses, so . . ." She consulted her list. "I'll check for spelling errors."

As I was glancing at my own list, my phone vibrated on my desk.

"Maybe Erin's finally calling to apologize," I said. "Did you say anything to her?"

"Of course not," said Leila. "You told me in private."

When I picked up my phone, the screen said Nicole.

"Hey, what's up?" I asked when I answered.

"Hi!" she said. "I was just wondering how the coding was going."

"Good, but slow," I said. I heard faint music through the speaker. "Are you playing *Wands and Weapons*?"

"Yeah!" Nicole's voice sounded surprised. "How did you know?"

"My friend Leila's playing, too!" I said. "She's going to kill the Troll King soon."

"Hopefully," chimed in Leila.

"Ooh, he's tough," Nicole said. "I still haven't beaten him." Then in a more excited voice, she added, "Does Leila want to fight him with me? I can meet her at the bridge!"

I looked at Leila. "Do you want to fight the Troll King with Nicole?"

"Yes!" Leila sat up straighter but then quickly dropped her shoulders. "Wait, we have to finish this code first."

Nicole, who must have heard her, said, "Oh, come on. You can take a break for a couple minutes."

I held up two fingers to Leila. "It'll only take a couple minutes."

"I don't know . . . ," said Leila.

"Tell Leila if someone else kills the Troll King before her, he won't re-spawn for hours," said Nicole.

I relayed the message to Leila, who finally nodded emphatically.

"Okay! Let me buy my dagger real quick."

Nicole spoke in my ear. "Tell her—"

"Why don't I just put you on speaker?" I asked with a laugh. I pressed a button on my phone, and Nicole's voice carried across the room.

"Hello?" asked Nicole.

"Hi!" said Leila and I.

After Leila bought her dagger and found Nicole's

character, I watched them battle a scary-looking troll. Just as Leila's assassin and Nicole's knight were about to die, Leila pulled a stealth move and vanished. She reappeared behind the troll and brought him to his knees with the Unwielding Dagger. Then Nicole sliced his head off.

We all cheered.

"That was so cool!" I said. "And sort of gross."

Mom opened the door and smiled down at Leila and me. "I take it you solved . . ." Her voice trailed off when she saw Leila's laptop screen. "What's this?"

Shoot. This required a craftily worded explanation.

"You see—"

"We killed the Troll King!" Nicole cheered from over the speaker.

Mom cocked her head to one side and pointed to my phone. "Who's that?"

"Oh, just Nicole," I said, trying to play it down.

"Hi, Mrs. Chung!" Nicole shouted.

Mom pressed her lips together and breathed air through her nostrils. Leila tried to make herself as small as possible.

"You're supposed to be working on your coding project but instead you're playing video games?" Mom blustered.

"Uh . . . Nicole, I have to let you go," I said.

"Okay, b—"

I hung up before she could say anything else that might get me grounded for life.

"We were just taking a little break," I said.

"I've heard noise coming from this room for the last thirty minutes," Mom informed me. Both Leila and I glanced at the clock.

Whoops.

"We're sorry, Mrs. Chung," said Leila. "It's my fault for pulling up the game."

Mom shook her head. "I have a feeling Nicole was behind this somehow. Did she talk you girls into playing?"

I didn't say anything, but Leila nodded.

"I thought so." Mom held out a hand. "Phone."

I sighed and handed it over.

"I'm also disconnecting the router," said Mom. "No games. Do your project."

"This isn't for a grade," I reminded her. "It isn't even for any of my classes."

"It doesn't have to be," she said. "You committed to something, and you should stick to it. And not let *anyone* keep you from it."

Of course. This wasn't about the project; this was about Nicole.

Mom closed the door without another word, and I made a face at it.

"Well, at least I killed the Troll King," said Leila.

"I'm sorry about that," I said, pointing toward the door. "She can be a little mean sometimes."

Leila shrugged. "She has a point. We were supposed to be working on this project."

I rubbed my hands together. "Okay, then let's debug this code, so I can show my mom we had time for work *and* play."

Twenty minutes later, our code was finally error free (we'd forgotten a parenthesis, misspelled *source*, and put in an extra curly brace).

"Well, it compiles, but we won't know if it truly works until we hook up the lights," said Leila.

"Hopefully Lucy and Sophia will have their code finished tomorrow so we can put all the pieces together," I said.

I walked with Leila to the front door, and she made sure to stop and talk to my parents, who were in the living room.

"Sorry again for earlier," she told them.

Mom smiled at Leila. "It's not your fault. But thank you for apologizing."

After I walked Leila out, I swaggered back to the living room and sat on the end of the couch.

"Well, we had time to play *and* debug our code," I said. "I think somebody owes somebody an apology." I pointed from Mom to me.

Mom snorted. "Forget it! If it wasn't for me, you'd still be playing."

"No, we wouldn't," I said. "Nicole was just helping Leila with that one quest."

Mom pointed to Oliver. "My husband, a former gamer, will now respond."

Oliver clicked his tongue. "You think it's only one quest, Maya. Then that turns into two. Before you know it, you've been playing all night."

"Maybe for you," I said, "but not for me and my friends."

Mom raised an eyebrow. "When I came to check on you, you had no idea how much time had passed."

My victory speech wasn't going at all how I'd planned. "My *point* is that you were mean, and you should apologize."

"And my point," said Mom, "is that you were doing your work just fine until Nicole called. She's a bad influence."

"Ugh!" I got to my feet and stomped off. "I am so sick of everyone thinking that."

"If everyone thinks it, that should tell you something!" Mom called after me.

I shut my bedroom door to block out her nonsense. Then I picked up Sophia's dress and a pair of scissors, cutting holes in the places she'd marked. When I finished, I needed to sew the edges of the holes so they wouldn't fray, so I dug through my closet for my sewing kit.

During my search I found a book of Mad Libs that Erin and I had filled in on our morning bus rides. I smiled as I read them, and when I reached the last page, I closed the book with a sigh.

I didn't like fighting with Erin. But I also didn't like that she'd done my part of the project.

I looked over the code she'd sent Leila and me to attach to our portion. I had to admit, it was pretty impressive. Except I wouldn't have abbreviated the variables for the light colors. It was easier to search for white, blue, and orange than the letters *W*, *B*, and *O*. Leaning over my keyboard, I clicked a few keys and edited the code so the words were spelled out. *Now* I'd worked on the first part like I was supposed to!

Feeling much better, I left my room and approached Mom with my most apologetic expression.

"Can I please use my phone?" I asked. "I want to call

Erin. I'll even do it where you can see me."

Mom studied me for a moment and then pointed to my room. "It's in your desk drawer."

I glanced behind me. "It was with me the whole time?"

Mom smirked. "Since you never use your desk, I figured you wouldn't look there."

Oliver turned away from the show he was watching. "Hey! It took me five hours to build that thing."

"I'll use it right now," I promised, hurrying away.

When I found my phone, there were several texts from Nicole, but I ignored them. Taking a deep breath, I dialed Erin's number. She answered on the first ring.

"Hello?"

"Hey," I said. "Can we talk?"

rin and I talked until bedtime. I apologized for getting so upset, and she apologized for not checking with me before she wrote my code. After I read a few of our old Mad Libs for a good laugh, Erin filled me in on her day.

"I finally found an outfit for the dance, and I'm trying out for another play!" she said. "Most of the roles are for guys—it's so frustrating! But I'm up for anything. I'll wear a beard if I have to."

"Good luck!" I told her. "They'd be crazy to turn you down."

"Thanks! I agree," she said with a laugh. "How was coding with Leila?"

"Great! Our section is done." I waited as Erin applauded, "I also watched her and Nicole play *Wands and Weapons*."

"Ooh! I love that game." Erin paused. "Wait. Nicole

came to your house, and your mom didn't throw her in the dungeon?"

I giggled. "Nicole didn't come over. She and Leila played over the phone."

"Gotcha. By the way, I like how you didn't deny having a dungeon," Erin said in a sly voice.

"I'll never tell," I said mysteriously.

When I finally hung up with Erin, I realized I hadn't gotten further on Sophia's dress than poking it full of holes. But at least I had Thursday and Friday to finish it.

The next morning, Erin produced a fresh book of Mad Libs for us to fill in on the bus.

"I asked my mom to pick it up last night," she said, flipping to the first page. "Give me a noun."

The entire trip to school we snickered and snorted, and we were still giddy when we got off the bus.

"I never thought the word *pineapple* could be so funny," I said, wiping my eyes.

Erin nodded. "I laughed so hard I almost pineappled my pants!"

At that, we both doubled over with laughter.

"Can't … breathe!" Erin fanned her face.

"Wow, I wish *my* bus rides were that fun," someone nearby commented.

I glanced over to see Lucy and Sophia watching us and grinning.

Erin thrust the book of Mad Libs at them. "You have to read these."

Lucy took the book but didn't open it. "Actually, first I need the code Maya and Leila worked on last night." She turned to me. "Can you email it to me?"

I reached into my backpack. "Even better, I can give you a flash drive. Erin's code is already attached to ours."

"Perfect! I'll add mine to the bottom, and we can test it in homeroom." She slipped the drive into her pocket. "And now for some pineapple-related humor."

Erin showed Lucy the spot in the book, and Sophia nudged me.

"How's my dress coming?" she asked with a giddy smile.

The dress I'd cut a hundred holes in and left draped over a chair?

"Great!" I lied. "It's almost done."

She clapped her hands. "Awesome! Do you think I could get it tomorrow?"

Lucy, who was reading the Mad Libs story, let out a very loud *ha*, which was exactly the sound I wanted to make . . . for a different reason.

"Tomorrow?" I repeated. "But the dance isn't until Saturday."

"I know," said Sophia, twisting her hands together. "But since it's my first dance, my cousin agreed to do my hair and makeup, and she wants to see the dress early for style ideas."

I shrugged. "It's just your blue dress. With lights."

"Yeah, but describing it isn't the same as seeing it, you know?"

I scratched my head. "But I don't have the code set up." To myself, I added, *Also, the dress looks like moths ate it.*

Sophia chewed her lip. "Okay, so just plug the dress into the wall and take a picture of it." She scrunched her nose. "Weirdest thing I've ever said."

Lucy and Erin giggled.

"Sure," I said with a nonchalant smile. "I'll do it when I get home."

But first I was going to have to sew the dress like mad. There was no way I'd be able to meet Nicole after school. She was going to kill me.

"I'll see you guys in homeroom," I told them, heading into the building.

Nicole was by her locker when I reached the seventh-grade hall, and she waved tentatively when she saw me. When I waved back, she smiled and hurried over, a pink, beribboned gift bag swinging at her side.

"I wasn't sure if you'd be mad at me for getting you in trouble," she said.

"So you thought you'd win me over with a gift?" I teased.

"Of course not!" Nicole held the bag out. "This is just a thank-you for being my friend. I haven't really made any others at this school."

I took the bag and peeked inside. "Ooh. Is it jewelry?" I lifted out a little white box and opened it. "It is!"

Coiled into a circle was a silver bracelet with a ladybug charm.

"Cute!" I said, taking it out of the box. "Why a ladybug?"

Nicole took the empty box and bag from me and put them in her locker. "Why?" Her forehead tensed for a moment and then relaxed. "Because they're the best dressed of all the bugs. Like you!"

"Aw, thanks!" I reached over and hugged her. "Will you help me put it on?"

"Of course! I'm glad you like it." Nicole hooked the bracelet on my wrist. "But if you don't, we can exchange it after school."

I winced. "About that. I can't hang out today after all."

Nicole's eyes widened and then narrowed. "You'd better be joking."

"I'm sorry, but—"

"What happened this time?" Nicole scowled. "Did your mom ground you? She's such a witch!"

Whoa.

Mom and I had our disagreements, but that was going a little far.

I stepped back and frowned. "That's not why I can't hang out, and don't ever call her that."

Instead of apologizing, Nicole quipped. "Please. I'm just saying what you're thinking."

"I would never think that about my mom," I said in a bristly tone. "And even if I did, it's not your place to say it."

Nicole held up her hands. "Fine. Then let me guess. You have to meet with *coding club.*" She said the last two words in a snarky tone.

At first I'd felt bad for canceling plans, but now Nicole was making me glad I had.

"No, it's not coding club, either," I said. "But if it was, so what? I told you this project was going to take up my time. It's important to me."

Nicole's hands went to her hips. "Oh, and I'm not? I'm a way better friend to you than the girls in that club."

"Why?" I crossed my arms. "Because you bought me a bracelet?"

"No! Because I support you and tell you all your dumb ideas are good."

My jaw dropped. "My *dumb* ideas?"

By this point we'd started to gather a crowd of onlookers.

"Yeah, a light-up dance floor?" Nicole gave a derisive snort. "Are you trying to make disco cool again?"

"You didn't seem to think it was such a dumb idea when I told you about it." I couldn't believe this was happening. "Now if you'll excuse me, I have to get to the library to work on my project for *coding club*." I imitated her snarky voice.

"You've changed, Maya!" Nicole shouted after me as I walked away. "You were a lot more fun when you used to steal stuff!"

I froze in my footsteps for a second, and people started to whisper. Then I kept going, raising my arm and waving so the ladybug charm jangled on the bracelet.

"Bye, Nicole," I called without looking back.

Hurried footsteps rushed up behind me, and I whirled around, ready to continue our argument. Instead, I found myself looking up, up, up at a tall girl who was frowning down at me.

"Let me see that bracelet."

I blinked up at her. "Excuse me?"

The girl grabbed my wrist. "Let me see it!"

I struggled to get free. "Let go!"

"This is mine," said the girl, tugging at the chain. "You stole it!"

"What?" I wriggled out of her grasp and stepped back. "You're crazy."

Lucy, who was passing by, ran over.

"Jill, what are you doing?" she asked the tall girl.

"She stole my bracelet!" Jill pointed at me.

The crowd who'd been watching me and Nicole was now watching me and Jill.

"I did not!" I said. "It was a gift from . . . someone." I hesitated to call Nicole my friend after the way she'd been acting.

"Yeah, it *was* a gift. From my grandma to me," said Jill, jabbing herself with a thumb.

"I didn't take it," I reiterated. "I would never do that."

Jill scoffed. "I literally just heard a girl say you used to steal stuff. Anyone else hear it?" Jill raised a hand and glanced at the crowd.

"*Used to,*" I emphasized. "And it was a bottle of nail polish. One time!"

My mom says: If you want people to wonder, start a rumor. If you want people to gossip, add details. I could already see a couple kids texting on their phones.

"Are you sure it's your bracelet?" Lucy asked Jill. "Maybe it just looks like yours."

"There's a tag near the clasp with my initials on it," said Jill. "J.A. And one of the links near the middle is bent."

Lucy helped me take the bracelet off, and we all inspected it.

There was a bent link in the middle and initials on the tag.

My heart dropped into my stomach.

"I'm so sorry," I told Jill, offering her the bracelet. She snatched it up. "Someone gave it to me, and I thought they bought it."

"Yeah, right," said Jill.

"It's true," Lucy piped up. "Maya wouldn't take something that wasn't hers."

I could've hugged her. She didn't even know the truth of what happened, but she was still on my side.

Jill grunted. "So who took it out of my locker, then?"

I could've said Nicole.

I should've said Nicole.

But the last thing the school needed was more gossip.

Also, I had a feeling Jill might turn Nicole into a smudge on the carpet.

"It doesn't matter. I'll handle it," I told her.

Jill stared me down. "You'd better. Because if anything else goes missing from my locker, I'm coming after you."

"So that was mildly terrifying," said Lucy as we entered the library.

"What was mildly terrifying?" asked Leila. She was unboxing a tiny blue LED bulb with steel pins poking out. Erin, who was unboxing an orange one, laughed.

"They're probably talking about Mr. Garcia shaving off his goatee," she said.

Sophia made a face. "That man has a lot of moles."

"No, not that. A girl from my math class threatened Maya just now," said Lucy.

Leila and Erin both froze.

"What?" asked Leila.

"Did you tell the principal?" asked Erin.

"I can't," I said. "Because I kind of deserved it."

I told them about Jill's stolen bracelet and added, "So now I have to talk to the person who gave me the bracelet."

"Nicole. Just say Nicole," Sophia told me. "We all know it was her."

My other friends nodded, and I sighed.

"Fine. Nicole, then."

"How did she get into Jill's locker to begin with?" asked Leila.

I rubbed my forehead. "Nicole works as an office aide. She told me she can get any locker combo, but I didn't think she'd use that power to steal something."

"You need to let the principal deal with her," said Erin.

I shook my head. "I want to try talking with her first." I pointed to Sophia. "Besides, we need to see if our lighting system works. Did you bring the setup?"

"I did, but we're gonna talk more about Nicole later." Sophia reached into her bag and fished out her phone. While she pulled up her music playlist, Leila and Erin plugged the LED bulbs into pin slots on the Arduino.

"I thought we were using Christmas lights," I said.

"We are for the real display," said Leila, "but they need special wiring since they use so much power, and Mrs. Clark said she didn't want us messing with the electrical system."

"So for this demo we're using these single LEDs that we can hook up directly to the Arduino. They'll flash like the Christmas lights, but on a smaller scale," said Erin.

Lucy powered up her laptop and uploaded the code to

the Arduino. "Okay! Code's ready!"

"Sensor's ready," said Sophia, switching it on.

"Lights are ready," Leila said.

"Here we go!" I said as Erin did a drumroll on the table.

Sophia pressed the PLAY button for a song, and music filled the room with a fast beat. We leaned forward in anticipation.

But the lights did nothing.

"Shoot," said Lucy.

Leila checked all the connections while the music continued to play. The lights didn't so much as flicker.

"Is there something wrong with the code?" asked Sophia.

Lucy pulled up the coding window on her laptop. "I didn't get any errors."

We all gathered around the laptop.

"Start at the beginning," I said.

"No way there's anything wrong with my code," said Erin. "My dad helped me write it."

"But it's also where we labeled all our light colors and pins," said Sophia. "If we don't have the variables matched to the right pins . . ."

"White is pin three, blue is pin five, and orange is pin seven," Lucy read while Leila checked the Arduino. "And the ground pins to return their electrical currents are four, six, and eight."

"Yes to all of the above," Leila said.

Erin scanned the laptop screen and leaned in closer. "Wait a minute. Did one of you guys change my code?"

"No," said Leila. "Why?"

Erin scrolled through our program until she got to Lucy's output section. "That's why!" She pointed to the screen. "*W, B, O*."

"You're gonna have to give us a little more," said Sophia with a confused look.

"I wrote my code with the initials *W, B*, and *O* and told Lucy to do the same," said Erin.

"Which I did," said Lucy.

"Right! But . . ." Erin scrolled back to the top of the page. "Someone changed my code and spelled out the colors. Lucy asked it to send output to *W, B*, and *O* when the pins are now labeled *White, Blue*, and *Orange*."

Leila snapped her fingers. "The variables don't match. It can't find *W, B*, or *O*."

"Exactly!" Erin said.

"Ohhh," Lucy and Sophia said.

"Oops," I said.

Everyone looked at me.

"You did this?" asked Erin.

I grabbed her arm. "I'm so sorry! I thought it'd be easier to read. I shouldn't have touched your code."

Erin laughed. "Maya, it's a quick fix. Don't worry about it."

"Really?" I asked. When Erin had done my part of the coding, I'd freaked out. Why was she being so understanding?

She nodded. "I'm just glad we figured it out before Mrs. Clark noticed."

"Well, we *think* we figured it out," said Sophia. "Let's make sure it actually works."

"On it," said Lucy, who was changing Erin's colors back to their abbreviations.

While she uploaded the changes to the Arduino, we *all* did a drumroll.

The lights started flashing to the different volume levels, and a moment later the music was punctuated with our cheers of joy.

"We did it!" cried Erin.

"We're brilliant!" I declared, high-fiving Sophia.

"And now you have the code for my dress!" she said with a broad smile.

I bit my lip. Since I'd been honest with Erin . . .

"I'm actually not as far along on the dress as I said," I told her, shrinking back a little.

Sophia's smile dipped. "Can you still have it done tomorrow?"

"Absolutely!"

Sophia shrugged. "Then, no problem."

Every muscle I'd been tensing relaxed. How was nobody upset with me?

"You're not mad?" I asked.

Sophia tilted her head to one side. "I can't really be, can I? You're doing me a huge favor."

Lucy, who happened to be standing nearby, added, "This is seriously cool of you to do for her, Maya."

I blushed and ducked my head, feeling a little embarrassed.

Nicole and I had been wrong. My friends *did* appreciate me.

Leila had listened and not said anything to Erin after I complained about her doing my code; Erin had been totally understanding when I messed with *her* code; Lucy had defended me; and now Sophia was being cool about her dress.

Maybe *I* had been the unappreciative one. And maybe Erin wasn't the only one who deserved to know what a good friend she was.

I threw my arms around Sophia. "You're so great!"

Sophia patted my back. "Um . . . thank you?"

I moved on to Lucy and did the same thing. Then on to Leila. When I got to Erin, she squeezed me tight.

"What's with all the love?" she asked when she finally let go.

"I just wanted you guys to know how much I value our friendship," I said.

"Awww," said Lucy, placing a hand to her heart.

Sophia smirked and asked, "Can you value our advice, too?"

I knew what she meant, and I knew she was right. They all were.

I had to tell Principal Stephens the truth about Nicole.

Chapter Ten

I really did have great friends. Lucy volunteered to talk to the principal with me since she'd witnessed the bracelet argument. I felt guilty betraying Nicole, but I also remembered how I'd felt when Nicole had broken into my locker. I couldn't let her do that to other kids.

Principal Stephens was kind, but concerned about the situation and assured me she'd talk to Nicole. That was one problem out of the way. Now I just had to finish Sophia's dress.

At the end of the school day, I practically vaulted down the bus steps when it stopped in front of my house. There was *so* much to do.

But as soon as I reached my driveway, I froze. There was a car parked there that didn't belong to either of my parents. It did, however, belong to Nicole's aunt.

I crept up the driveway and opened our front door a crack. Three distinct voices. My mom was talking to Liz and Ash in the kitchen. I slipped into the house and as close to the kitchen as possible. Liz and Ash had their backs to me, and Mom was out of my line of sight.

"She shouldn't take all the blame for stealing it," said Liz.

"She shouldn't take *any* of it," said Mom.

I sucked in my breath. They were talking about the bracelet!

I probably shouldn't have been surprised that the principal would call Nicole's aunts. But I *was* surprised that Mom was defending Nicole.

"I think we can agree she's not the best influence," said Ash. "If she could admit her part in this—"

"No," said Mom in a flat voice. "My daughter had nothing to do with it."

My mouth fell open. Mom wasn't defending Nicole; she was defending *me*. And Nicole's aunts were trying to say I was the reason Nicole was a troublemaker!

I prepared to storm into the kitchen, but as I walked into Mom's eye line, her eyes flitted to me for a second, and she gave a subtle shake of her head. I retreated into the living room where I could still hear everything but wouldn't be seen.

"Nicole hasn't gotten into any trouble until she started at this school," said Liz. "And the other day Nicole told me Maya suggested she put photocopied pictures of their faces in all the school windows."

That was a joke! I wanted to yell.

"I'm sure Maya was joking," said Mom.

If she'd been standing right next to me, I would've hugged her.

"I also found a candy wrapper in Nicole's pocket, and she said Maya made her steal it," said Ash.

I grabbed a pillow off the couch and squeezed it. Four M&M's. I had four M&M's out of the bag that Nicole chose to steal. I listened close for Mom's response.

"How convenient that Maya's always there when Nicole needs someone to blame."

If Mom had been holding a microphone, it would've been the perfect time to drop it and walk away.

Nicole's aunts didn't say anything for a moment. Finally there was a sound of chairs scraping across the kitchen floor.

"Clearly, we're not going to get through to you," said Liz. "Maybe it's best if the girls don't spend time together."

"I one hundred percent agree," said Mom.

I heard them coming and ducked behind the couch

until Mom said goodbye to Liz and Ash and closed the door behind them.

"Come out, come out, wherever you are," Mom sang.

I popped up and said, "I didn't steal that bracelet or tell Nicole to steal it."

Mom smiled. "I know."

I approached her with my hands behind my back. "I want to say something, but I don't want you to gloat."

"Oh, sweetheart." She put her arms around me. "I can't promise that."

I laughed. "Fine. You were right about Nicole. I should've listened."

Mom squeezed me and, thankfully, didn't gloat. "I know you wanted to believe she was a better person."

"I did," I agreed.

"But as long as she doesn't think she's doing anything wrong, that can't happen." Mom held me at arm's length. "Which is why I know you didn't have anything to do with the bracelet. After you got caught stealing the nail polish, you knew you were wrong."

"So maybe I helped Nicole by turning her in," I said with a hopeful smile.

Mom sighed. "Maybe. But if her aunts won't believe she's guilty, maybe not." She made a face. "And I'm sorry, but now I really have to forbid you from hanging out with Nicole. I think Oliver will agree."

"I do, too," I said, leaning into Mom for another hug. "But thanks for giving her a chance. And for believing in me."

"You're welcome." Mom released me. "Other than that bit of drama, how was school?"

"Good! My friends and I got the lights to blink in time to music." I showed her a video I'd taken.

"Wow! Good job!" She gave me a high five. "How about we celebrate with dinner on the town?"

I gasped. "Really? That would be—"

I thought of a video of Sophia saying, "I can't wait to see my dress do this!"

I groaned and slumped. "Can we do it another night?" I pointed to the video. "I have to finish Sophia's dress."

Mom stroked her chin and asked, "How about I bake your favorite cake instead?"

I popped onto my tiptoes and kissed her cheek. "You're the best!"

She stepped aside so I could get past her. "I'll let you know when dinner *and* dessert are ready."

Now that I was back in performance mode, I hurried to my room and tossed my backpack in the corner. Picking up Sophia's dress and my sewing stuff, I found a comfy spot on my bed and some fast music on my phone. Then I got to work reinforcing the holes I'd cut in the dress.

An hour and five position changes later, I realized I wasn't even halfway done. I'd reinforced twenty holes—at this rate, I wouldn't be done with the basic stitches for four hours. Then I still had to poke the lights through and stitch *them* into place. And after that, I still had to put together the elements to make the lights blink.

I glanced at my clock, which was a little blurry since I'd been staring so closely at the stitches. If I stopped to eat dinner, I wouldn't be done with this dress until after midnight.

I needed to sew faster.

But doing something faster with a sharp object is never smart, and in a matter of seconds, I'd stabbed the needle into one of my knuckles.

"Ow!" I shrieked, dropping the dress and grabbing my hand.

Footsteps pounded up the stairs, and Mom threw open my door. The smell of chocolate wafted into the room.

"What? What happened?"

"I stabbed myself with a needle," I said, sucking on my knuckle.

"Let me see." Mom took my hand and watched the blood

pool. "It's not bad, but we need to bandage this so you don't bleed on Sophia's dress."

"I don't have time to stop," I said. "Can you patch it up while I keep sewing?"

I picked up the needle between my thumb and index finger and forced it through the fabric. Mom called to Oliver to bring the first aid kit while she held my injured finger above my head to slow the bleeding.

"Why don't you take a break?" she asked. "Dinner's almost ready."

I shook my head. "No time. There's so much to do, and food will just slow me down."

"It'll also give you energy," said Mom, taking the first aid kit from Oliver, who stood in the doorway.

"Ouch," he said. "Were you trying to sew yourself into the dress?"

"Something like that." I stopped Mom. "No, don't use a big bandage. I need to be able to use both hands."

She found a smaller one and applied it. "If you don't want to eat in the kitchen, at least let me bring you something."

"Mom," I said, looking her in the eye. "Every time I have to pick up a fork is time I don't have a needle in my hand."

Mom didn't blink. "Maya, you have to eat."

"Fine," I said, switching the needle to my now-bandaged hand. "Then I'll sew with this hand and eat with the other."

Oliver watched me jab a needle through the fabric. "I don't think that's a great idea. You might end up with a fork in your dress and a needle in your face."

Mom chuckled but stopped when I scowled.

"Seriously, you guys. I don't have time," I said.

Mom sat beside me. "What if we help you?"

I raised an eyebrow. "You know how to sew?"

She crossed her arms. "Who do you think made your baby clothes?"

"A machine in a factory."

She rolled her eyes. "I meant the ones we *didn't* buy from the store."

"Oh," I said. I held up the dress. "You think you can do stitches like this?"

"Yes," she and Oliver both said.

I gave him an incredulous look. "You sew, too?"

He looked mock offended. "Just because I'm a guy, you don't think I can? When I was in college, I had to mend holes in my shirts. And my socks. And even my pants."

Mom looked at him. "Were you the Incredible Hulk or something?"

It was my turn to laugh. "Okay, okay. You guys can help," I said.

"Dinner first." Mom reached for my hand.

While we ate, I filled them in on what I still had to do for the dress.

"So how do the lights know when to blink?" asked Oliver.

"The code my friends and I programmed will pick up on the audio signal and turn it into a pattern for the lights," I said. "It's not quite what we're doing for the display at the dance, since that's using the different volume ranges, but the basic idea is the same. I'm only using one color of lights for Sophia's dress, though."

"And once we sew the lights into the dress, you hook them up to a circuit board or something?" Mom asked.

"Exactly," I answered.

"But how will it get power?"

"From a battery pack," I said. "I'll sew it into the shoulder of Sophia's dress, where it won't be as noticeable."

Oliver shook his head. "This is amazing stuff, Maya. I have to say, I'm impressed."

I beamed at him. "Thanks!"

"We're raising quite a clever girl," Mom agreed.

I danced a little bit in my chair. "Can we please have more dinners like this?" I asked. "Where everyone says all these good things about me?"

Oliver and Mom laughed.

First, they'd offered to help me with the dress, and now they were praising me for the work I'd been doing. It wasn't just my friends who appreciated me. My family did, too! And if *they* could appreciate *me* . . .

I tapped my fork against the side of my drinking glass. "I'd like to make a toast," I said, standing and raising my glass.

My parents exchanged an amused look but did the same.

"To Mom and Oliver," I said. "Thank you for always supporting me and doing your best with a sometimes difficult child. Cheers!"

"Cheers!" they both said.

"What do you mean *sometimes* difficult?" Oliver added.

I pretended to splash him with my drink, and Mom laughed.

"Come on. Let's put away these dishes so we can finish that dress," she said, reaching for my dirty plate.

"I'll get them," I said, taking hers instead.

Mom drew back. "You're offering to do chores?"

"Well, yeah." I stacked Oliver's plate on top of the others. "If you can help me, I can help you."

"Aw, that's nice," said Oliver. "That makes me want to help you even more."

"Really?" I asked. "With what?"

Oliver grinned and pushed back his chair. "With your dessert." He dashed into the kitchen, and I glanced at Mom.

She grabbed the plates from me. "Take no prisoners," she said, arming me with a fork.

I raised it like a spear and chased after Oliver.

Because as much as I appreciated my loved ones, I also appreciated chocolate cake.

As promised, the next morning I delivered Sophia's dress, which she couldn't even wait until after school to try on. While my friends and I set up our light show in the library with Mrs. Clark's help, Sophia disappeared into the librarian's office and changed into her dress.

"First, we'll give you a preview of the lights display," I told Mrs. Clark. "And then after that, Sophia's dress."

Mrs. Clark rubbed her hands together. "I can't wait!"

When Sophia came out, Leila turned off the library lights and Erin started the music. Instantly, the display lights flared and faded to the music. Even though my friends and I had tested the LED lights several times, we were still excited to see the Christmas lights work. We cheered along with Mrs. Clark.

"Wonderful!" she said, applauding. "You girls have done an amazing job."

Erin stopped the music, and the room darkened.

"Now we'll be switching off the display and switching on Sophia!" I announced as my friends giggled. "Are you ready, Sophia?"

"Ready!"

I activated the battery pack on her shoulder, and Erin started the music again. For dramatic effect, I'd had her choose a song that held its opening note for ten beats so everyone could see the dress all lit up.

The reactions were not disappointing.

My friends all gasped and squealed, including Sophia, who hugged herself and twisted from side to side to make the radiant skirt billow around her.

"I love it!" she cried.

"Soph, put your arms down! You're blocking the lights," I said with a laugh.

"Sorry!" she shouted as the music picked up and her dress began to flash in time to the song. There was more cheering, and Erin squeezed my shoulder.

"Dude! This is awesome." Her smile was lit by the

flickering bulbs of Sophia's dress.

"I'm just glad to see her so happy," I said, nodding to Sophia, who was now hopping around with Lucy.

Mrs. Clark put a hand on my other shoulder. "You've done a wonderful thing here."

I could've hugged myself and danced like Sophia at the compliment, but I knew I didn't deserve all the credit.

"Actually," I said, "the code for the dress is a modified version of the one we wrote for the dance. So Leila, Erin, Lucy, and Sophia did a wonderful thing, too."

My friends cheered at the mention of their names, until Mrs. Clark laughed and told us to settle down. We quieted, and Erin turned off the music while Leila flipped on the overhead lights.

"So what do you think of our display for the dance?" Erin asked Mrs. Clark.

"Does it make you think of the future?" added Lucy.

"It sure does." Mrs. Clark smiled broadly. "And in the hands of you five, the future is very, very bright."

Chapter Eleven

*N*ormally I hate the school gym because it means sit-ups and smelly clothes. But on Saturday night, I almost leaped from the car when Mom pulled up in front of it.

"We're here!" I exclaimed, opening my car door.

"You're still wearing your seat belt," Mom reminded me.

"Oh, right." I laughed and unbuckled it.

"Um . . . Maya? I have a small problem." In the seat behind me, Lucy squinted through one eye while a set of false eyelashes dangled over the other. "They're falling off."

"Shoot! I knew I should've used more glue."

I reached back and carefully adjusted Lucy's eyelashes with the tips of my fingers.

Lucy blinked a few times, and the lashes stayed.

"Yay! Let's go!" she said.

Blowing Mom a quick kiss, I grabbed my purse and hopped out of the car. "We'll see you in a couple of hours!" I called as Lucy and I ran toward the gym.

"Don't kiss anyone!" Mom called back.

She and Erin's mom must have been part of the same *don't-let-your-kids-kiss* club.

When Lucy and I entered the building, it was almost empty, which was what I'd expected. The dance committee was putting up decorations, and my friends and I were arriving early to set up our display. Except for Sophia. I'd told her to show up a little after the dance started, so she could make a grand entrance.

Across the gym floor, I spotted a girl in red tights and a blue tunic that had a gold foil lightning bolt across the front. She was tacking a string of lights to the wall.

"Hey, Leila!" I nudged Lucy, and we hurried to join our friend. "I love your costume."

She glanced at us and widened her eyes. "Maya, your dress is way more awesome in person! I love the mirrors."

"It's a little awesome," I agreed, holding my index finger and thumb close together.

"And, Lucy, you look great, too!" said Leila.

"Thank you!" Lucy said with a small curtsy. Her dress was covered with planets and stars.

Leila pointed at Lucy's dress. "Your idea of the future is . . ."

"Space exploration," said Lucy, stepping back to study the light display. "I think you need more orange over there." She pointed to one side, and I helped Leila drape some orange bulbs over a bare spot.

Suddenly, near the gym entrance a cellphone blared "Hail to the Chief," the president's fanfare. Leila, Lucy, and I all looked over to see Erin wearing a pantsuit and carrying an American flag. As she approached us, she waved to an invisible audience with a toothy grin. The rest of us hooted and clapped.

"The future is female politicians! I love it!" crowed Lucy.

"It's perfect," I agreed. "But, Erin, I thought you wanted to wear something to match Jeremiah."

"I am! He's dressed as a Secret Service agent." She tucked her American flag into her jacket pocket and studied our handiwork. "The display's looking pretty good!"

"Yep. Just a few more lights to string up," said Leila.

"Well, let's get to it," said Erin. She flicked her jacket collar and raised an eyebrow. "That's an *executive* order."

I groaned, and Lucy giggled.

"Yes, Madam President," said Leila.

After we finished hanging our display, we hooked up the

sensor and Arduino system to the relay board with help from the custodian.

"Should we test the lights?" I asked, after we'd plugged them into the relay board. I reached into my purse and pulled out a tablet computer. "I have an app on this thing that'll show us sound fluctuations, and we can compare them to the lights."

"Yes! But we need the perfect song," said Lucy, running to the DJ table. We chased after her and watched her beg the eighth-grader who was DJing to let us see his playlist.

Leila and Erin joined Lucy behind the table, and I stood on the opposite side, looking at the song titles upside down.

"What about this one?" I pointed to a song.

"Too slow," said Erin. Her finger went down the list. "This one?"

"Not enough quiet beats," said Leila. "I vote for the one under it."

I nodded. "That's a good one! I'm going to the back wall so I can film our light display after I test it."

Erin picked up a headset and passed it to me. "Use this to talk to us."

"Hey!" said the DJ.

Leila rolled her eyes. "It's the school's equipment, Derek, not yours. And we only want to borrow it for one song."

"Maybe two," said Lucy with a big smile, picking up another headset.

I giggled and put mine on. "Okay, I'll let you guys know when I'm ready," I said, jogging across the room.

Once I was in position, I opened the sound-visualizing app and spoke into my headset mic. "Give me five seconds, and then play it loud!"

Lucy gave a thumbs-up from across the room and started a countdown on her fingers.

I pulled my phone from my dress pocket and set it up to record.

A moment later, rock music flooded the room.

And once again, the lights worked perfectly, matching the app on my tablet note for note.

Students started trickling into the gym, and many were drawn to our light display. They took pictures of it and with it before wandering to the dance floor or the punch bowl.

And then Sophia walked in.

Her hair and makeup were flawless, and her dress twinkled like a sky full of stars. Beside her, Sammy was grinning from ear to ear, but not at the people crowding around the two of them. He only had eyes for Sophia.

"Aww!" Lucy's voice sounded in my ear.

We all rushed over to Sophia.

"You look so beautiful!" Leila told her.

"Stunning," I agreed.

"Who do you think can fit more chips in their mouth, me or Jeremiah?" was Erin's contribution. Her date was smiling, too, with potato chips falling from his lips.

I was about to comment when I spotted another person by our light display. Except this time I didn't squeal with joy.

Because it was Nicole.

She glanced over at that exact moment, no doubt feeling my eyes on her. I wasn't sure how to react. Should I wave an open hand of peace? A clenched fist of defiance?

Nicole lifted a hand and waved me over. It wasn't friendly *or* hostile, but my palms felt clammy just the same.

"Want me to go with you?" Lucy asked.

I shook my head. "I can handle her," I said, and strode toward Nicole with more confidence than I felt.

"I know what you did," Nicole said as soon as I was in earshot.

She let her words dangle in the air, as if waiting for an apology. But I couldn't give it.

"I had to," I said. "Your actions hurt people more than you think."

Instead of arguing with me, Nicole lowered her gaze to the gym floor. "Yeah, my aunts were pretty mad when they found out."

"And a girl threatened me when she thought I stole her bracelet," I said.

"I heard." Nicole hunched her shoulders. "I didn't want either of those things to happen. And I don't want to put anyone else through it."

I took a hopeful step toward her. "So change! Be better."

She gave an exasperated sigh. "I've tried. But nobody pays attention to me when I'm Good Nicole."

"You did all those things so people would notice you?" I asked.

Was it possible she felt unappreciated like I had?

She nodded. "But people haven't noticed. Not the way I wanted."

I thought for a moment and pointed at myself. "Look at my dress."

Nicole frowned. "Maya, I don't think this is the time to talk fashion."

I held my skirt out so she could see her image in all the mirrors. "Just *look*. See your reflection?"

"Yeah. So?"

"So the future is *you*," I said. "And you can either let

it be a bad one or a good one."

Nicole's forehead wrinkled. "But I don't know how to make it good."

"You did bad things and got negative attention. Guess what happens when you do good things?"

The corners of Nicole's mouth curled up. "You think so?"

I glanced past her to the kids talking with Sophia. Sophia was smiling and pointing to me and my friends.

"I know so," I said.

Nicole scrunched her nose. "Well . . . I guess I could try."

"I admire your enthusiasm," I said with a wry smile. "How about starting small? Maybe apologize to Lucy and Sophia for trying to bully them."

"But—"

I nudged her in Lucy's direction. "Go."

As Nicole wandered over to Lucy, Erin hopped over to me and bumped my hip with her own.

"Everything okay?" she asked.

"Just trying to get Nicole to deliver some overdue apologies." I glanced at Erin's empty hands. "No fruit punch?"

"One of the chaperones took away my punch privileges!" she said with a frown. "If there's a five-cup limit, they should mention that on the flyer."

I laughed. "Where's Jeremiah?"

Erin leaned closer and said, "Getting me another cup."

I wagged a finger at her. "Watch out. You're gonna cost him *his* privileges."

Leila bounded over in her superhero costume. "Point that finger somewhere else!" she said to me. Then she turned to Erin. "It's okay, Madam President. I've got you."

Ever the actress, Erin pointed to me and shouted, "Put the freeze on her, Ms. Marvel!"

I held up a hand. "Why am I a villain?"

"You're right!" declared Erin. "Nicole Davis is the real villain."

"Actually, she might not be," said Lucy, joining us. "You guys won't believe this, but she just apologized to me!"

"Really?" I asked with a smug smile. I spotted Nicole in the crowd as she was walking away from a puzzled Sophia.

Sophia said something to Sammy and then made a beeline for the rest of us.

"That was weird," she said. "Nicole told me she was sorry she'd been rude to me."

Lucy pointed to herself. "Me too!"

"That *is* weird," said Erin. "Do you think she meant it?"

"She looked pretty uncomfortable," said Lucy. "So I'd say yes."

Sophia looked over her shoulder. "You know, if you would have asked me yesterday what Nicole's future was, I would've said trouble," she said. "Now I'm not so sure."

"The future's always changing," Leila mused.

"It is," I said, looking at my circle of friends. "But I'm glad I have you guys for whatever comes next."

Erin put an arm around me. "Me too."

"Yeah," said Lucy.

"I wouldn't have it any other way," said Sophia with a smile.

"We are pretty awesome," said Leila. "I mean, look at what we created!"

The five of us faced our light display and watched it pulse to the music while all around us kids danced, sang, and laughed. It felt good to be part of the reason they were happy, and it made me think of so many other things we could do.

But that could wait until tomorrow. Tonight I was going to have fun with my friends.

And maybe enjoy some watered-down punch.

Acknowledgments

Always, always, always for family, friends, fans, and God.

For my husband, Ari, who is my tech genius and sanity checker.

For my agent, Jenn, who always encourages me to write what I want.

For my editor, Eve, who knows having fun is as important as learning something new.

For my GWC advisor, Jeff, who is a master of simplify, simplify, simplify.

Don't miss these other Girls Who Code books!